Who Will Run the Frog Hospital?

Who Will Run
the Frog Hospital?

a novel by

LORRIE MOORE

Alfred A. Knopf

New York

1994

THIS IS A BORZOI BOOK
PUBLISHED BY ALFRED A. KNOPF, INC.

Grateful acknowledgment is made to the following for permission to
reprint previously published material:
CPP/Belwin, Inc.: Excerpt (in Franglais) from "Theme from New York, New York,"
words by Fred Ebb, music by John Kander, copyright © 1977
by United Artists Corporation, c/o EMI Unart Catalog I. International copyright secured.
Made in USA. All rights reserved. Worldwide print rights controlled by
CPP/Belwin, Inc., Miami, Florida 33014. Used by permission.
EMI Music Publishing: Excerpt from "And When I Die" by Laura Nyro, copyright © 1966
(copyright renewed 1994) by EMI Blackwood Music Inc. (BMI); excerpt from "Tapestry" by
Carole King, copyright © 1971 by Colgems-EMI Music Inc. (ASCAP).
International copyright secured. All rights reserved. Used by permission.

Frontispiece illustration, *Who Will Run the Frog Hospital?*, by Nancy Mladenhoff

Library of Congress Cataloging-in-Publication Data
Moore, Lorrie.
Who will run the frog hospital?: a novel / Lorrie Moore.
p. cm.
ISBN 0-679-43482-8
1. Teenage girls—New York (State)—Fiction.   2. Friendship—
New York (State)—Fiction.   I. Title.
PS3563.O6225W58   1994
813'.54—dc20   94-278
CIP

Manufactured in the United States of America
First Edition

for MFB

How public—like a Frog—
To tell one's name—the livelong June—

EMILY DICKINSON

I am thankful that this pond was made deep
and pure for a symbol.

HENRY DAVID THOREAU, *Walden*

Well run, Thisby.

WILLIAM SHAKESPEARE,
A Midsummer Night's Dream

In appreciation of their notice and support I would like to thank the Guggenheim Foundation, the American Academy of Arts and Letters, Brandeis University, the Wisconsin Arts Board, and the University of Wisconsin.

For her work and her permission, my deepest gratitude goes also to Nancy Mladenoff.

Who Will Run the
Frog Hospital?

IN PARIS we eat brains every night. My husband likes the vaporous, fishy mousse of them. They are a kind of seafood, he thinks, locked tightly in the skull, like shelled creatures in the dark caves of the ocean, sprung suddenly free and killed by light; they've grown clammy with shelter, fortressed vulnerability, dreamy nights. Me, I'm eating for a flashback.

"The grass is always greener on the other side of the fence," says Daniel, my husband, finger raised, as if the thought has just come to him via the *cervelles*. "Remember the beast you eat. And it will remember you."

I'm hoping for something Proustian, all that forgotten childhood. I mash them against the roof of my mouth, melt them, waiting for something to be triggered in my head, in empathy or chemistry or some other rush of protein. The tempest in the teacup, the typhoon in the trout; there is wine, and we drink lots of it.

We sit beside people who show us wallet pictures of their children. *"Sont-ils si mignons!"* I say. My husband constructs remarks in his own patois. *We, us, have no little ones.* He doesn't know French. But he studied Spanish once, and now, with a sad robustness, speaks of our childlessness to the couple next to us. "But," he adds, thinking fondly of our cat, "we do have a large *gato* at home."

"*Gâteau* means 'cake,'" I whisper. "You've just told them we have a large cake at home." I don't know why he always strikes up conversations with the people next to us. But he strikes them up, thinking it friendly and polite rather than oafish and irritating, which is what I think.

Afterward we always go to the same *chocolatier* for whiskey truffles. One feels the captured storm in these, a warm storm under the tongue.

"What aggrandizement are we in again?" my husband asks.

"What 'aggrandizement'?" I say. "I don't know, but I think we're in *one of the biggies.*" My husband pronounces *tirez* as if it were Spanish, *père* as if it were *pier*. The affectionate farce I make of him ignores the ways I feel his lack of love for me. But we are managing. We touch each other's sleeves. We say, "Look at that!," wanting our eyes to merge, our minds to be one. We are in Paris, with its impeccable marzipan and light, its whiffs of sewage and police state. With my sore hip and his fallen arches ("fallen archness," Daniel calls it), we walk the *quais*, stand on all the bridges in the misty rain, and look out on this pretty place, secretly imagining being married to other people—right here in River City!—and sometimes not, sometimes simply wondering, silently or aloud, what will become of the world.

WHEN I WAS a child, I tried hard for a time to split my voice. I wanted to make chords, to splinter my throat into harmonies—floreted as a field, which is how I saw it. It seemed like something one should be able to do. With concentration and a muscular push of air, I felt, I might be able to people myself, unleash the crowd in my voice box, give birth, set free all the moods and nuances, all the lovely and mystical inhabitants of my mind's speech. Afternoons, by myself, I would go beyond the garden and the currant bushes, past the lavender-crowned chives and slender asparagus, past the sunflowers knocked bent by deer or an unseasonal frost, past the gully grass to the meadow far behind our house. Or I'd go down the road to the empty lot near the Naval Reserve where in winter the village plow and dump truck unloaded snow and where in summer sometimes the boys played ball. I would look out upon the wildflowers, the mulch of swamp and leaves, the spring moss greening on the rocks, or the boulderous mountains of street-black snow, whatever season it happened to be—my mittens clotted with ice, or my hands grimy with marsh mud—and from the back of my larynx I'd send part of my voice out toward the horizon and part of it straight up toward the sky. There must have been pain in me. I wanted to howl and fly and break apart.

The result was much coughing, wheezing, and a hoarseness troubling, I was told by Mrs. LeBlanc, our cleaning woman, to hear in a child. "You getting a cold, Miss Berie Carr?" she might ask when I came in too soon for dinner. She would say my name like that, making it sound Irish, though it wasn't. "Nope," I'd say brusquely. She was jolly, but also bearish and oniony; I didn't like her breathing close; I didn't want her inspecting me like a nurse. We could scarcely afford a cleaning woman, but my mother was often lonely for talk, even in our crowded house, and she liked to sit with Mrs. LeBlanc in the kitchen, over cigarettes and tea. Even when I didn't see Mrs. LeBlanc, even when I'd successfully avoided her, I knew when she'd been there: the house would be full of smoke and still messy except for the magazines in new, neat stacks; my mother would be humming; the check on the counter would be gone.

After a year, when the chords I wanted consistently failed to appear, and all I could make was a low droning rasp to accompany my main note (where was the choir of angels, the jazzy jazz?), I finally stopped. I began instead to wish on spiderwebs or five-sided stones. I wished for eternal and intriguing muteness. I would be the Mysterious Dumb Girl, the Enigmatic Elf. The human voice no longer interested me. The human voice was too plain. It was important, I felt, to do something fancy. I just didn't know what.

Although no voice was ever plain in our house—not really. Even if it took practically my whole life, until the summer I was fifteen, for me to see that. There were fancinesses: Years of my mother's Canadian French slipping out only in the direst of lullabies. Or the faux-patrician lilt her voice fell into when she wanted to seem smart for her redoubtable in-laws—her voice became a trained one, trying to relocate itself socially and geographically. Or years of my father's college German *fired* across the dinner table, as my mother would try apprehensively to learn it this way, in order to talk with him at supper about private matters—without the children catching on. *"Was ist los, schätzchen?"*

"Ich weiss nicht."

We would sometimes have students from other countries living with us for a few weeks, sleeping on one of the Hide-A-Beds—in the living room, cellar, or den. Sometimes there were teachers—from Tunisia, Argentina, or Tanzania, countries with names that sounded like the names of beautiful little girls. There were South American city planners, African refugees. "My parents were trying to shock the neighborhood," I would say years later, at social occasions when one was supposed to be able to speak of one's upbringing and be amusing at the same time.

Everything in our house when I was young felt cloaked with foreignness, code, mood. People would come and stay, then go.

One of the many results of this for me was a tin ear for languages. My brain worked stiffly, regrouped and improvised sounds. For a while I believed Sandra Dee was not only an actress but one of the French days of the week. I sang "Frère Jacques" with the bewildering line, "Sonny, lay my Tina." Knowing that a foreign tongue was often tense marital code, off-limits to the *kinder*, all forbidden chirp and wind, belonging to the *guests*, I grew sullen, and vaguely deaf, resentful in a way that was at the time inexplicable to myself; I tuned out. I played with my food—the heavily cerealed meat loaf, the Habitant soup and blood pudding, the peeling fish sticks—or else I ate too much of it. I stuffed my mouth and clutched my stomach, chewing. From early on and for a long time thereafter when I heard something not English—Mr. Gambari's Ibu, Mrs. Carmen-Perez singing a Spanish song—as a form of politeness my brain shut down. My teachers in school—French, German, Latin—would call on me, but I couldn't hear what they were saying. I never knew what it was—their mouths just moving and the sounds reaching me, jumbled and scary.

• • •

Later, when I was an adult, someone at a dinner party played me a recording of Asian monks who could indeed split their voices, create a shattered, choral sound that was like being oneself but also so many others. It was a choir of brokenness, lamentations. It wasn't pretty, but it reminded me again, right there at that dreary meal—everyone pronouncing on Marx, Freud, hockey, Hockney, mugged liberals, radicals with phlebitis, would Gorbachev soon have his own Hollywood Square?—it reminded me of the sound I might have managed if my efforts had succeeded. It reminded me of how children always thought too big; how the world tackled and chiseled them to keep them safe.

Certainly "safe" is what I am now—or am supposed to be. Safety is in me, holds me straight, like a spine. My blood travels no new routes, simply knows its way, lingers, grows drowsy and fond. Though there are times, even recently, in the small city where we live, when I've left my husband for a late walk, the moon out hanging upside down like some garish, show-offy bird, like some fantastical mistake—what life of offices and dull tasks could have a moon in it flooding the sky and streets, without its seeming preposterous—and in my walks, toward the silent corners, the cold mulchy smells, the treetops suddenly waving in a wind, I've felt an old wildness again. Revenant and drunken. It isn't sexual, not really. It has more to do with adventure and escape, like a boy's desire to run away, revving thwartedly like a wish, twisting in me like a bolt, some shadow fastened at the feet and gunning for the rest, though, finally, it has always stayed to one side, as if it were some other impossible life and knew it, like a good dog, good dog, good dog. It has always stayed.

The summer I was fifteen I worked at a place called Storyland with my friend Silsby Chaussée, who all this is really about. Storyland was an amusement park ten miles outside our little village of Horsehearts, a quarter mile from the lake. Its theme was storybook characters, and there were installations and little enactments depicting nursery rhymes—Hickory Dickory Dock or Little Miss Muffet—as well as fairy tales. Snow White. Hansel and Gretel. There were rides and slides. There was the Old Woman Who Lived in a Shoe, which was a large purple boot you could climb to the top of, then coast down its aluminum tongue into a box of sand. There were the Three Billy Goats Gruff—an arced redwood bridge, a large plaster troll, and three live goats, who could be fed rye crisps purchased from a dispenser. There was the Jungle Safari section, with its floating rope bridges and submerged, fake crocodiles. There was Frontier Village, with its fake ghost town and the local high school boys dressed up as cowboys. Finally, there was Memory Lane, a covered promenade between the exit and the gift shop, lined with gaslit street lamps, and mannequins dressed in finery— moth-eaten bustles and top hats—then propped precariously against antique carriages. Sometimes on rainy days Sils and I would eat our lunch in Memory Lane, on one of the park benches placed along the walk. We were conspicuous and out of place—half mimes, half vandals. But most of the tourists smiled and ignored us. We sang along with the tinny, piped-in music, whatever it was—usually "After the Ball" or "Beautiful Dreamer"—but sometimes it was just the Story-land theme song:

> *Storyland, Storyland—*
> *not a sad and gory land.*
> *But a place where a lot*
> *of your dreams come true.*
> *Books come to life and nursery rhymes do, too.*

Storyland, Storyland:
Bring the whole famil-lee!
(And Grandma-ma!)

The coda about Grandmama, hovering there in some kind of diminished seventh chord, like the comic soundtrack to a cartoon—waa-waa-waa—always made us grimace. We would sing along, our mouths full of sandwich, then open wide to showcase our chewed-up food and our horror at the thought of our grandmothers there, in the park, somehow standing in line at one of the rides. *And Grandmama!*

Eeek!

Sils was beautiful—her eyes a deep, black-flecked aquamarine, her skin smooth as soap, her hair long and silt-colored but with an oriole yellow streak here and there catching the sun the way a river does. She was hired by the Creative Director to be Cinderella. She had to wear a strapless sateen evening gown and ride around in a big papier-mâché pumpkin coach. Little girls would stand in line to clamber in and tour around the park with her—it was one of the rides—then be dropped back off next to a big polka-dot mushroom. In between, Sils would come fetch me for a cigarette break.

I was an entrance cashier. Six thousand dollars came through a single register every day. Customers complained about the prices, lied about their children's ages, counted out the change to double-check. *"Gardez les billets pour les manèges, s'il vous plaît,"* I would say to the Canadians. The uniform I wore was a straw hat, a red-and-white striped dress with a flouncy red pinafore over it, and a name tag on the bodice: Hello My Name Is Benoîte-Marie. I'd sewn nickels into the hem of the pinafore to keep it from flying up in breezes, but besides that there was nothing much you could do to make the dress look normal. Once I saw a girl who'd been fired the year before driving around town still wearing that pinafore and dress. She was crazy, people said. But they didn't have to say.

In summer the whole county was full of Canadian tourists from over the border in Quebec. Sils loved to tell stories of them from her old waitress job at HoJo's: "I vould like zome eggs," a man said once, slowly looking up words in a little pocket dictionary.

"How would you like them?" she'd asked.

The man consulted his dictionary, finding each word. "I would like zem . . . *ehm* . . . on zee plate."

That we were partly French Canadian ourselves didn't seem to occur to us. *Sur le plat.* Fried. We liked to tell raucous, ignorant tales of these tourists, who were so crucial to the area's economy, but who were cheap tippers or flirts or wore their shirts open or bellies out, who complained and smoked pencil-thin cigars and laughed smuttily or whatever—it didn't matter. We were taught to speak derisively of the tourists, the way everyone in a tourist town is. In winter we made fun of the city people who came north to Horsehearts' Garnet Mountain to ski. They wore bright parkas and stretch pants and had expensive skis, yet could only snowplow. They screamed when they fell, wept when their skis released and sped off down the trail. We would zoom by them in our jean jackets and jeans and old tie boots. We would smirk and hum Janis Joplin songs, descend into the quiet of the trees, with our native's superiority—our relative poverty, we believed, briefly, a kind of indigenous wit.

At Storyland, when Sils—Cinderella herself!—came to fetch me for a smoke, I would shut down my register, let one of the ticket tearers watch over it for me, and then go off with her, into the alley between Hickory Dickory Dock and Peter Pumpkin Eater's Pumpkin, where we'd haul out a pack of cigarettes and smoke two apiece, the Sobranies and Salems that made us feel gorgeous and wise. Sometimes our friend Randi, who was Bo Peep and had to wander through the park carrying a golden staff and wearing white ruffled pantaloons and a yellow-ribboned bonnet (moaning to the children, "Where are my sheep? Dears, have you seen my sheep?"), joined us on a quick break.

"Have you seen my fucking sheep?" she'd ask, stepping into the alleyway (or Memory Lane if it was raining and lunchtime), hitching up her pantaloons, the elastic to which always itched her. Ten years later Randi would have a nervous breakdown selling Mary Kay cosmetics; she would stop selling them but keep on ordering them, letting them pile up in boxes in her basement; instead of selling, she'd go out, get drunk in the backseat of her car, and pass out. But now, here, a smoking Bo Peep, she was tireless, ironical, and young. "I was hoping I'd find you gals here." She'd take quick puffs, then walk out, her skirt sometimes still hiked up in the back. "Randi, you've got a great ass," Sils would say, checking her out.

We had to be on the lookout for Herb, the park manager. (What did all these little children think when Cinderella and Little Bo Peep turned out to have nicotine stains and so much cigarette smoke on their breath? my husband, a medical researcher, asked me once, and I shrugged. Different things, I mumbled. Different times. Everybody smoked. Their parents smoked.)

"You haven't seen my sheep? Why, I've lost them and don't know where to find them!"

Randi's voice trailed off, and Sils and I hummed songs we knew, ones we'd learned in Girls' Choir at school—medieval Christmas carols, a section of the Brahms German Requiem, the duet from *Lakmé*, the theme from *The Thomas Crown Affair* (Miss Field would be so proud!)—or songs we'd heard on the radio that week, ones we learned from songbooks, lots of Jimmy Webb. Sils liked "Didn't We," Dionne Warwick's version, and at home was learning the chords on her guitar. " 'This time we almost made our poem rhyme.' " She made the chord changes in the air, like weaving, with her left arm stuck out like a neck. "Yeah, yeah, yeah," I said. "Et cetera, et cetera." But I sang, too, warming to its prettiness.

I did the alto harmony. That was always my part. Rummaging about beneath the melody, trying to come up with something low and nice, something supportive—decorative but deep.

Afterward I'd light a cigarette and say nothing.

"I had a girl this morning who kept petting the glitter on my dress, staring up at me all agog, you know, like this." Sils slumped her shoulders, dropped her jaw.

"Did you swat her?" I asked.

"I beat the shit out of her," she said.

I laughed. So did Sils, and when the low bodice of her dress moved a little, I tried not to look toward her breasts, which as they sometimes rose into light or fell back into shadow fascinated me. I was flat, my breasts two wiener-hued puffs, and I had to avoid all dresses with darts, all nylon shirts and plunging bathing suits. Though I pretended otherwise, I hadn't even menstruated yet, though I was already fifteen. The words "developed" and "undeveloped" filled me with dread and loathing. "When you develop," my mother might begin a long, embarrassing prophecy, or the school nurse would come to talk to us in Science, and I would freeze in my chair, not moving a muscle, trying to disappear. It seemed a mortifying truth that no one but I could admit to that I was never going to "develop." But I tried to manage my disappointment: I hadn't wanted to be a freak, mostly I'd just wanted to grow breasts so I could look at them. I'd wanted to study them, powder and perfume them. Now I had to accept facts: I'd been bypassed by Mother Nature, the garlanded and white-robed figure whom I sometimes saw on margarine commercials, summoning thunderstorms. I'd been overlooked by her.

And so I told long self-deprecating breast jokes about myself, relying on such analogies as fried eggs, bug bites, bee stings, animals or tin cans run over by a car, pancakes, pencil erasers, doilies, and tacks; breasts were still a curiosity to me. It had been only a few years before that Sils and I would examine at great length any centerfold we could get our hands on, or W. T. Grant underwear ads, or even Land O Lakes butter, cutting out the Indian maiden from the package and bending the knees so that they appeared like breasts through a slot we made in her chest. We'd laugh in a fascinated, obscene way. We were obsessed with breasts. We'd stuff washcloths, teacups, golf balls, tennis balls, cotton balls in our shirts. Once we made her mother, who was long divorced and worked late hours as a receptionist at the Landmark Motel, show us hers. She was a sweet and guilt-ridden mother, exhausted from her older sons (their loud band practices in the basement; their overnight girlfriends; their strange, impermanent, and semiannual treks across the border to Canada to avoid the draft, though their numbers were high; the spaghetti they hung on the porch as a "wind chime"; the snapshots they taped to the inside of the refrigerator, pictures of what the dog had done to the trash). She was fearful that in trying to make ends meet she hadn't shown enough attention to her little daughter, so when we began to chant "Show us your breasts, show us your breasts!," strangely enough, she did. She lifted her sweater, unhooked her bra, and shook them loose, looking out at us in a confused way, as we stared at them—veiny, and dark, and amazing.

But now it seemed it was only me. I was the only one still obsessed.

The late spring sun had freckled the upper part of Sils's chest, and her silky hair, rinsed in cider and beer, was shiny as Christmas foil. "I kept asking her, So what's your name?" said Sils. "Where do you go to school?—you little twerp—Do you like your teacher? Things no real Cinderella would ever say, but there was a spell on with this girl."

"That couldn't be disspelled." This was the sort of boring cleverness I was prone to, a skinny, undeveloped girl good in school.

"She kept asking me about the prince. She's not *two*. You'd think she'd get it. *Ceci n'est pas une pipe.*" Sils had memorized all the slides from History of Art. "There is no prince."

I smoked Sobranies down to the poison-gold filter. I exhaled through my nose like a dragon. "*Now* you tell me," I said. "You're *not* really Cinderella?" We were never very witty as girls, but we thought we were. Our idea of a funny joke was to refer to our chins as "The Happy Acre Pimple Farm." In a town where everyone said things like "Jeesum Crow" and "sheeesh," we said "fuck"—but in a daring, private way. "What the fuck, babe." Sils liked to say that, with a smirky, smoke-frayed laugh. I would say it, too. Once, in eighth grade, her forehead broke out and she tried to shave the pimples off with a razor. It wasn't funny at the time—her forehead bled for a week—but when we wanted later to laugh, we would summon it up: "Remember the time you shaved your forehead? What the *fuck*, babe," and we'd fall on the floor. We looked to secret things. We looked to stories and misadventures and mined them for their narcotic ore. We loved to laugh violently, convulsively, no sound actually coming out until suddenly we'd have to gasp in a braying way for breath.

Now she gave me the finger with one hand and then with the other balanced her lit Sobranie against her thumb. But she smiled. She shrugged. She hummed. She said, "Listen," and then belched out the carbonation from her Fresca. She was my hero, and had been for almost as long as I could remember. In being with her—cigarette break to lunch to cigarette break—I got through the dull days.

We'd started working at Storyland in May, on the weekends, through the Memorial Day rush, until school let out in early June. Then we worked six days a week. Up until then we had met during the school week in the cemetery to smoke. Every day we would have what we called a "cemetery lunch." I would clamber up over the hill, past the blue meadow of veronica and flax, past the broken stick-arbor and the Seckel pear, down the gravel path, into the planked swamp and on up to the gravestones, where Sils would be waiting, having arrived from the other end. She lived on a small oaky street that dead-ended into the cemetery (next to which she lived). "Is this street symbolic or what?" Sils would say to anyone who visited. Especially the boys. The boys adored her. She was what my husband once archly referred to as "oh, probably a *cool* girl. Right? Right? One of those little hippettes from Whositsville?" She could read music, knew a little about painting; she had older brothers in a rock band. She was the most sophisticated girl in Horsehearts, not a tough task, but you have to understand what that could do to a girl. What it could do to her life. And although I've lost track of her now, such a loss would have seemed inconceivable to me then. Still, I often surmise the themes in her, what she would be living out: the broken and ridiculous songs; the spent green box of Horsehearts; the sad, stuck, undelivering world.

That spring we usually met at the grave of Estherina Foster, a little girl who had died in 1932, and whose photograph, tinted with yellows and pinks, was fastened to the stone. There we would shiver and smoke, the air still too cold. We'd list against the other gravestones, lean forward and brush hair from each other's face. "Hold still, you've got a hair."

Were we just waiting to leave Horsehearts, our friends, enemies, our airless family lives? I often think that at the center of me is a voice that at last did split, a house in my heart so invaded with other people and their speech, friends I believed I was devoted to, people whose lives I can only guess at now, that it gives me the impression I am simply a collection of them, that they all existed for themselves, but had inadvertently formed me, then vanished. But, what: Should I have been expected to create my own self, out of nothing, out of thin, thin air and alone?

But what do I mean "they"? Perhaps I mean only Sils. I was invaded by Sils, who lives now in my vanished girlhood, a place to return to at night, in a fat sleep, during which she is there, standing long-armed and balanced on stones in the swamp stream, stones in the cemetery, stones in the gravelly road out back. How I resented the boys coming, as they did. I resented it early, even the hint of it. They were sneering and injurious and uninterested in me. They hooked their thumbs through their belt loops. More obsessed even than we with the fluids and failings of the body, they told long ugly jokes, ones with loud refrains like "plugging in" or "coming in handy." They owned BB guns and shot the frogs in the swamp, not always killing them right away. Sils and I, stupid and young, would bring tweezers from home and, pushing through the cattails and the gluey pods of the milkweed, would try to seek out and save the poor frogs—digging in through their skin, pulling the BBs out, then bandaging the squirming, bleeding animals with gauze. Few of them lived. Usually, we would find the frogs dead in the watery mud, the gauze unraveled about them, tragically, like a fallen banner in a war.

The week she was hired as Cinderella, Sils made a painting of this, what we'd done with the frogs those years before. She painted a picture in deep blues and greens. In the background, through some trees, stood two little girls dressed up as saints or nurses or boys or princesses—what were they? Cinderellas. They were whispering. And in the foreground, next to rocks and lily pads, sat two wounded frogs, one in a splint, one with a bandage tied around its eye: they looked like frogs who'd been kissed and kissed roughly, yet stayed frogs. She framed it, hung it in her bedroom, and titled it *Who Will Run the Frog Hospital?*

By that time, Sils had a boyfriend—a boy named Mike Suprenante from glamorous, forbidding Albany—and the painting's meaning had become larger, broader, funnier; it had become everything.

She'd met Mike in late March, up at a lake bar called Casino Club, where we'd gone dancing. We had fake IDs and on weekends during the school year it was a good place to dance. Sometimes we danced with each other—boyless and defiant, with a tight, parodic pout. We would do the twist in a deeply satirical way. We would jitterbug, twirling under each other's arms. We then waited for the men to buy us drinks. The dance floor was large and platformed; the bands were loud, winking, and friendly; the drinks were cheap on Ladies Night, and sometimes we would see our student teachers there, young and handsome in navy sport coats. Sometimes one of them would ask Sils to dance, not recognizing her immediately, and then in the middle of the song realize who she was and give her an embarrassed "Hi" or a sheepish shrug or point his fingers like a gun her way or else at his own head.

The night Sils met Mike, she was wearing a fake peony in her hair and a long sleeveless tunic and jeans. She wore all her rings and bracelets on one hand, one side, skipping the other, leaving it bare. I danced a lot. Every time a guy headed our way to ask Sils to dance, Mike (a "handsome nondescript person," I said of him later), who had just walked over and introduced himself earlier that night, would swoop down with extra drinks and take possession of her, steer her back out onto the floor—he'd claimed her, "gotten dibs on her," and she'd let him. On fast dances with him, she did her intensity dance: she sank deeply into each hip and held her fists up in front of her (one ringed, one naked) like a boxer. Her face—with its long nose cut like a diamond, her cheekbones flying off to either side in a crucifix—looked stark and dramatic in this light. And so, by the time the other guys got to the table, finished swashing their gums with their beer, finished gulping, there was no one there but me. "Well, would *you* like to dance," they'd say, looking gypped. I didn't care. I understood. I'd worn my white earrings that glowed in the black light of the bar; I'd circled my eyes with shadow. I'd brushed my hair over my head and then thrown it back so that it was wild and full. I'd checked myself out in the ladies' room mirror: I was too skinny, and I wasn't Sils. But I was of the conviction—a conviction I held on to naïvely, for years—that if somebody got to know me, really know me, they'd like me a lot.

On the slow dances, like "Nights in White Satin," I let the men—construction workers, car salesmen—hold me close. I could feel their bellies and their sweat smell, their hard groins, their damp shirts, their big arms around me. Sometimes I'd rest my hands on their hips, my eyes shut and pressed into one of their shoulders while we danced.

"That was nice," they'd say at the end, shouting it over the band's next song.

"Thank you," I'd say. "Thank you very much." I always thanked them. I was grateful, and I let them know.

"How we getting home?" I yelled into Sils's ear—the standard question on our nights out. I was staying overnight at her house, one of the few ways I'd have gotten to remain out so late. Her mother had night duty at the motel, and her brothers were staying with their various girlfriends or else were in Canada again, Sils wasn't sure these days. She looked at me in a bemused way, shrugged, and pointed discreetly at Mike. He was tapping his foot, smoking a cigarette, and looking at the band, but he had his arm around her chair.

Why did I have to ask? I could always count on Sils; Sils was the way; Sils was our ride home, always.

Mike only had a motorcycle, but he'd borrowed a car from a friend. He drove slowly to make it last, kept looking at Sils, who sat next to him in the front seat, kept asking her questions like "How'd you get so beautiful?" To which she'd say, "Give me a break," and then laugh. I sat wordlessly in the back, looking out the window, watching the night trees and the darkened houses float by like boats.

Mike pulled down to the end of her street, right up into the entrance to the cemetery, and I got out and waited. I walked away from the car, to let them kiss. I had a lot of patience, I felt, for certain kinds of things. I hopped the low fence and roamed around the edge of the cemetery a little, but when I looked back, they were still in the car, kissing, so I walked farther out. I looked for little Estherina Foster's grave, and then sat there with her in the dark. I listened for a voice that might be hers, some whisper or peep, but there was nothing. I fiddled with a long-stemmed plastic rose that had gotten mashed there in the dirt. I brushed the mud off it, and bounced it around, tracing words in the air—my name, Sils's name, Estherina's name. I couldn't think of other names. I wrote *Happy Birthday*, *Fuck You*, and *Peace*. Then I tossed the flower away, into the shadows. How silent the

world was at night, the unbudded trees etched eerily into the
sky, the branches reaching as if for something to hold and
eat—perhaps the dead and candied stars! The ground was
cold, thatched with leaves; the nearby swamp had begun un-
thawing its sewagey smells. In the moonlight the sky seemed
wild, bright, and marbled like the sea. People alone, trapped,
country people, all looked at the sky, I knew. It was the way
out somehow, that sky, but it was also the steady, changeless
witness to the after and before of one's decisions—it wit-
nessed all the deaths that took people away to other worlds—
and so people had a tendency to talk to it. I turned away,
sitting there, hugging my legs, pulling my jacket close. I
plucked my earrings off and stuck them in my pocket, the
cool air strangely still and mushroomy. I wondered whether
I would ever be in love with a boy. Would I? Why not? Why
not? Right then and there I vowed and dared and bet that
sky and the trees—I swore on Estherina Foster's grave—that
I would. But it wouldn't be a boy like Mike. Nobody like
that. It would be a boy very far away—and I would go there
someday and find him. He would just be there. And I would
love him. And he would love me. And we would simply be
there together, loving like that, in that place, wherever it
was. I had a whole life ahead. I had patience and faith and a
headful of songs.

"Where've you been?" asked Sils. She and Mike were now
out of the car but leaning against it sexily.

"For a walk."

Mike turned toward Sils. "I should get this car back."

"Bye," she said.

He kissed her again, in front of me. "I'll phone you tomorrow," he said. He got in the car and did a three-point
turn—I'd been learning those at school, in Driver's Ed—and
then he zoomed away.

In the kitchen we fixed a quick, late-night breakfast: saltines and hot chocolate made from Bosco. We dipped the crackers in the hot chocolate and let them get soggy and float there, like gunk in a pond.

"Once in third grade," said Sils, "I didn't want to go to school, so I chewed up a bunch of saltines, kept them in my mouth and went upstairs, groaning, and spat them at my mother's feet."

"So attractive!" I said, and we giggled in an exhausted way.

"It worked." She was dreamy-eyed, drowning the crackers in her cup with a spoon.

"Ingenious," I said. I hoped she would glance up from her drink, look at me, say more. But she didn't.

Later, sprawled on top of the covers on her bed, which was a mattress on the floor of her room, Sils let out a long, satisfied sigh. At the foot, in the dim light of the little lamp she kept on when I was there, I lay curled in a sleeping bag and looked at her, beginning with her toes: the rubbery blue nexus of veins on top of her feet, the tendons splayed like the bones of a fan, the discolored sheen of the nails shimmery and vague as mother-of-pearl. The nuts and bolts of her were always interesting. She saw me looking.

"You've got wild toes," I said.

She yanked one foot toward her chest. "Did I ever show you these?"

"What?"

She examined her foot studiously. "In my toenails you can see Napoleon Solo and Illya Kuryakin."

"What are you talking about?" I pushed deeper into the sleeping bag and pretended to laugh at her.

"I'm serious," she said. "You can see their faces." She lowered her foot. "I'll show you tomorrow." She sighed again, thinking of Mike, I was sure. "Thanks, Berie," she said.

"For what?"

"For whatever." Then she fell completely to sleep, and in the low light for a while I watched my own shadow against the wall, a lumpy mountain range thrusting up peaks and crashing them again to avalanche and rubble, in a long, long restlessness that finally preceded sleep.

Often when I went over to Sils's house, she would have the side door unlocked and a salad or a cottage cheese sandwich waiting for me on the kitchen counter. A salad! A cottage cheese sandwich! How odd in memory to conjure it, the dressed cucumbers and celery assembled as if by a wife for her husband; or the sandwich, sweet and sloppy with mayonnaise. I would take it, eat it, then go upstairs to her room and sit next to her, strum the guitar with her, singing harmony to folk songs like "Geordie" or "The Water Is Wide I Cannot Get O'er," feeling myself a goner in the minor-seven chords, their sad irresolution stirring in me something lost and heartbroken, though how could that be, I was only fifteen. Still, something deeply sad had been born buried in me, stirring occasionally inside like a creature moving in sleep. Often I found myself concentrating on the frog painting, entering it with my eye, as if it were perhaps a dreamy illustration from a real-life fairy tale, or a secret passageway into another secret passageway. A joke into a secret joke into a secret. When we were younger, Sils and I had always looked for caves together, or some small undiscovered duck pond with ducks. We'd go to the Grand Union and cheer on the lobsters who had managed to break free of their rubber bands. We'd build a half-tent out of three open umbrellas and we'd get underneath it and play cards. We'd walk miles to the county dump to see the bears. By the time we were twelve, we'd bike to the head shop and buy wisteria incense. Or we'd go downtown to the Orpheum, say we were sixteen and see an R-rated movie, occasionally a foreign one, which would mesmerize and perplex us. We'd eat Junior Mints and popcorn—each candy a sweet pillow on the tongue; each popped corn as big and complicated as a catalpa bloom. On a dare we might even drink the blueberry punch, which was the color of Windex and shot up the sides of the Jet-Spray cooler like some wonder of nature; no one else in our town had ever drunk it. That's what the man behind the counter always said. We would wash it down with water from the lobby fountain. Then we would sit in the dark, on the left, to watch the movie from an angle, eyes peeled for flesh. At thirteen, we would hang out at W. T. Grant's, buying bras and ice-cream sundaes, and trying on men's sweaters, the bottoms of which, when we wore them at school, stretched out shapelessly, the hem warped and hanging around by our knees: that was the look we wanted. At fourteen, we would claim to be sleeping over at each other's house, and then we'd stay out all night, go to the railroad tracks, and from old mayonnaise jars drink liquor collected from our parents' own supply. Then we'd sleep in the family station wagon in the driveway, wake early, get donuts at Donna's Donuts at dawn when both the raised and glazed ones were still warm.

But increasingly now I was alone with my outings, wondering what it was like for Sils with her boyfriend Mike, what they did together, what were all the things I didn't yet even know to ask, and, now that she had gone to a new advanced place I hadn't, whether she liked me less.

In some ways my childhood consisted of a kind of wasting away, a wandering dreamily through woods and illegally in the concrete sewer pipes, crawling, or pleasantly alone in the house (everyone gone *for an hour!*) chewing the salt out of paper bits, or hiding under quilts in the afternoon to form a

new place somehow, a new space that had never existed before in the bed, like a rehearsal for love. Perhaps in Horsehearts—a town named for an old French and Indian War
battle, one full of slaughtered horses whose bodies bloodied
the village pond and whose hearts were said to be buried on
Miller Hill just south—the only things possible were defer-
ment and make-believe. My childhood had no narrative; it
was all just a combination of air and no air: waiting for life
to happen, the body to get big, the mind to grow fearless.
There were no stories, no ideas, not really, not yet. Just
things unearthed from elsewhere and propped up later to
help the mind get around. At the time, however, it was liquid, like a song—nothing much. It was just a space with
some people in it.

But one can tell a story anyway.

One can get a running start, then begin, do it, and be
done.

Things, I know, stiffen and shift in memory, become
what they never were before. As when an army takes over a
country. Or a summer yard goes scarlet with fall and its ve-
nous leaves. One summons the years of the past largely by
witchcraft—a whore's arts, collage and brew, eye of newt,
heart of horse. Still, the house of my childhood is etched in
my memory like the shape of the mind itself: a house-shaped
mind—why not? It was this particular mind out of which I
ventured—for any wild danger or sentimental stance or lunge
at something faraway. But it housed every seedling act. I
floated above it, but close, like a figure in a Chagall.

Before we had renovated our house, it had only one bathroom for the entire family and often I would rush to use it,
finding the line three kids deep; there was a mirror in the hall
and we used to clutch our groins and hop around, watching

ourselves, hoping we wouldn't explode. There were only two bedrooms for three children—the yellow room and the blue room. For a while my foster sister LaRoue, and my brother, Claude (in Horsehearts, pronounced *clod*), and I took turns sharing. Because LaRoue had first arrived at our house with another foster child who no longer lived with us—a slow, quiet girl named Nancy who had been beaten retarded by her mother—the two of them shared a room until Nancy went away, and then LaRoue was left with her own. I don't think I ever actually knew why or where Nancy went; our house was always inhabited by people other than us, all camped out on the Hide-A-Beds. That's why I'd sought Sils early, when I was nine, found her right there in my homeroom, alphabetized next to me, in the *C*s, and attached myself to her.

One May someone just came and got Nancy and took her away. It seemed scary to me, that that could just happen. That someone could simply come and take you and go.

But LaRoue stayed and got her own room—the blue one with its deep white windowsills—and called my mother "Mom." I was three years younger, though only one grade behind her, and I had the larger, yellow room with my brother Claude with whom I was close, being just a year older than he. Claude and I were "bunk-buddies," a phrase I used laughingly, ironically, bittersweetly, later in life, with lovers, those nights of an affair I'd sleep with a man but sexlessly, feeling tired, the dumb dog of my body too exhausted for love, running all week in the meadows of it, now desiring merely to sleep, beat, next to someone else but close, like a brother, like Claude. "Bunk-buddies: we can be bunk-buddies."

There was actually a bunk my brother and I slept in— sometimes he on top, sometimes I, to equalize things, I suppose. While the house was full of strict bedtimes and rules, all posted to the refrigerator with Bryson Paper Mill magnets, little pine trees with BPM stamped on them in gold, we were essentially unwatched children. We could find ways to do what we wanted, though we made a great deal of the moment at night when one of our parents (we were told, we assumed) would come in to check on us before they went to bed. We were never awake for this moment, but we knew of it, believed in it in a religious way, and sometimes, put to bed too early on a crickety summer evening, we'd prepare for it, like the Last Judgment. We turned it into a kind of body sculpture contest, posing in elaborate ways on our beds— standing on one foot, head hanging off one edge, arms lifted in the air and mouths and teeth and eyeballs arranged in astonished grimaces. "This will really surprise Mom," we'd say, or "Dad'll get a kick out of this," and then we'd try to fall asleep that way. In the morning we'd awake sprawled in ordinary positions, never recalling whether we'd glimpsed a parent or not, or how we had finally fallen off to sleep in this more normal way.

Claude was my first pal, before Sils, and we were each other's best friend, bunk-buddy, child spouse, until I was nine and he was eight, and we got separated—in a way, for the rest of our lives. We were too old; it was unseemly for a brother and sister to share a room. So the house got renovated, and each of the children got their own room—mine was downstairs, alone, off the first-floor hall. His was upstairs.

Soon afterward Claude befriended a new boy down the road, Billy Rickey. I stumbled around, then looked and found Sils, and that was that. Claude and I never really saw each other again, not in a true way. Passing each other in the corridor at school, seeing each other at dinner, then years later at holidays, weddings, and at funerals, we couldn't figure out who the other one was anymore. It was as if one of us had grown flippers or feathers or a strange stripe up the side, our species suddenly unclear.

But he always remained, for me at least, my first love, my child bride, and in a busy family, speaking in tongues, it was important to be married, somehow, to someone. So I was, had been, for a while, to Claude.

It was LaRoue who was alone. As little children, Claude and I were all bodies and sleep and play—closer than even adults usually get—and we'd viewed our parents as stern, distant royalty and LaRoue as older, disturbed interloper, visitor, rent-a-girl, but Christianly tolerated. Our family read the Bible every night at the dinner table, my father proceeding chapter by chapter through the Gospels, The Acts, the letters from Paul to Timothy (I imagined Paul Zabrowski at school and his annoying friend Timothy Wilson), through First John, Second John, Third John, all the way to Revelation ("And to the angel of the church in Philadelphia . . ." *Philadelphia?* Aunt Mimi lived in Philadelphia!), all the long strange verses, as we watched our food grow cold. And so we learned forbearance.

("We used to read the Bible at the dinner table, too," said my husband when I first met him and we were trading tales. He was Jewish, Socialist, half Hungarian.

"Really?" I'd asked.

"Yeah," he smiled. "Only we would read it in these really sarcastic voices." I laughed in a loud, honking way. We needed to joke and play. We were nervous, unsure. "What's also interesting," he said, encouraged to the point of derangement, "is that although most people called him God, we called him—well, we called him 'Fuckhead.' " Daniel slapped his hand across his heart. "One nation, under Fuckhead."

I fell sideways, hysterical, then tried to straighten, relocate my napkin, when our grim waiter began to approach. "At any rate," I said, stressing the oxymorons, "Bible reading and Peruvians on the Hide-A-Beds. That was my 'Family Life.' Be that as it may.

"Be," I added uncertainly.)

LaRoue existed for us as a gently tolerated and lonesome guest. She was fat where we were thin, blonde where we were dark. The thick pelts of our eyebrows shrieked across our faces, some legacy of the Quebec fur trade. Hers were faint and wispy, like an aerial shot of grain. She was older, separate, glum, periodically in some state of convalescence the details of which our parents did not reveal. Claude and I had staked out a separate contract. When people were gone, we explored their rooms. We'd get home from school early, our father still at work at BPM downtown—or "downstreet," as we used to say; at the mill he was head of the forest management department. Our mother would be at some steering committee meeting for the United Women Proposing the Beautification of Horsehearts—racking up minute notes about petunias and elms with Hilma Johnston, Thelma LaRose, Betty Dreiser, Lou-Anne Gerard.

LaRoue, after school, was usually at the Saddle and Riding Club.

And so Claude and I stepped in and went through stuff: my father's slacks hung by the cuffs from the top dresser drawer; his old wooden shoehorns like puppets on the closet floor. My mother's drawers full of sachets and girdles, and in the clutter on the dresser top the bright coral lipsticks and Avon colognes and old tinted photographs of herself when she was in college and had won Ankle Contests. In this way we gathered information about our parents; we were true and successful spies, for our parents never gathered much about us, we believed, nor cared to, in the way that was so often the case in large families of that time. My father could not even recognize me in a group, couldn't pick me out in the annual class picture—"Dad, that's not me, that's Cynthia Odekerk!"—never recognized us on his way to work when he passed my brother or me in a group of children heading to or from school. "Who?" "Cynthia Odekerk!" He walked, hatless and lost in thought, down through the village toward the river, where the mill was—"Hello, hello!" we'd call, and he would wave to us in a general, uninterested way, still moving with his big shoes and long stride, not really even looking up. "There's your father," a friend might say. Or, "That's *your* father?" as baffled as we.

I suppose we felt less bullied by his neglect than by his attentions, which tended to take the form of correcting us when we hit a wrong note on a Brahms piano intermezzo. "Aow!" he would yowl. "C-sharp, C-sharp, C-sharp!"

If we cried, he would say firmly, "Stanch and starch the mush!"

He started calmer conversations with us when it had to do with the crossword puzzle he was doing; he would call us to his side in the den, if he needed the name of a TV show he'd never seen. Once you'd given him the name of the show, he would ignore you again, turn back to the puzzle, and leave you standing there talking about the show a little, the various characters in it, what had happened to them, and what you thought would happen to them next. You'd be standing there talking to no one.

Nonetheless, we adored him. If he didn't know us, love us, even recognize us, it wasn't because he was invested elsewhere in other children. We had no rivals for his affection, except perhaps Brahms, Dvořák, the daily crossword, and our mother—and even then, not often her. In his iconic way our father remained very much ours. And in the long shadows of his neglect, we fashioned our own selves, quietly improvised our own rules, as kids did in America, in the fatherless fifties and sixties. Which was probably why children of that time, when they grew up, turned out to be such a shock to their parents.

No doubt some part of us, of course, remained obediently reduced and cowed by our lack of a deeper possession of him, by the inattention, no matter how we thought we had resourcefully accommodated it. But these were lessons and deformities perhaps more conspicuous in adulthood than in childhood, where we were often obstreperous and eager for battle; we had faces and jeers and impudent hand signals, our eyes rolling, our hands quacking at our sides when a grown-up spoke. But later, for years, I referred meekly to any strongly felt and informed opinion, or weeks and weeks of my own research, as "my two cents' worth."

C-sharp, C-sharp, C-sharp!

In public my grown brother muted his own fiercely forged self to a collection of apologies and excuses and if-you-don't-minds. Somehow we fell back from our original willful midnight constructions into ordinary, passive positions, mysteriously and in no time. Still we believed we could resume the other whenever we pleased, the Hieronymus Bosch, the artful splay, the Zappa arabesques, waiting for someone to walk in and see us like that and at last know who we really were deep down.

C-sharp!

Our father was unquestionably an impressive, solitudinous, autocratic figure. He had grown up in a family of cellists, Germanophiles, had even visited Germany in 1930, when he was ten; he had seen Hitler in a hotel lobby and was dazzled. But when all that celebrity and fine music played itself out so badly in history, he retreated with his passions, became a Baptist, listened, transported, to symphonies and tried to remember his children's names. We loved him, in the inexplicable, snobbish way of children: he was the tallest and most intelligent father in all of Horsehearts—this was generally acknowledged—and that seemed at the time all we or any other child ever really needed of a dad. We took our cues from our mother, who admired him to the point of debilitation; she was "brought up to do that with men," as she herself eventually came to declare. But we, as kids, did likewise. Sometimes I can still make my eyes well up—like a kid's game of fainting at will—thinking of how much I wanted him to like me. Though any adult can do that, make themselves wail like babies for the love that as children they had desired so, sought so, distorted themselves so to get but never got. I once rode eighty blocks with a cabbie who kept saying over and over, "And he never *hugged* me, and he never *kissed* me," until by Eighth Street he was weeping and I had to get out. It was unbearable.

Once, when I was nineteen, I gave my father a Father's Day card meant for uncles and neighbors. "You've Been Like a Father to Me," it read. His distance from us had become something of a family joke, but to him, staring at that card, it was unutterable and a shock; I don't know what I was thinking—that he'd laugh too?—I don't know, but the look of hurt that came across his face stunned me, confused me, sent me out for a striped tie and a different card: one with a demented sort of glitter and the word "Dad" writ large.

Years later, however, I grew angry; taking inventory of all he'd said and done, I came to think of him, bitterly, as a kind of Nazi. I was studying history. When I married a Jew, I waited for him to say something vague and dark, but he didn't. He was courteous and formal, not uncharming. My husband, upon meeting my father, encountering for the first time his towering blend of Fred MacMurray, Fred Gwynne, Fred Astaire—all the Freds—whispered to me in a panicked way, "Your father is such a *Father*. An *über*-Father. The mother of all fathers."

"Yeah," I said, smiling. "The mother of all fathers."

Sils was not really in love with her boyfriend, Mike, I was sure of it. I could tell it. He was tiring her out. You'd see them together: he all grinning and bursting, all raring to go, like an Irish setter, a tense dog, too much energy shining at the mouth, and she, exhausted from the night before, used up a little, unable to keep pace with this nineteen-year-old boy and his apartment, his revving motorcycle, his plans. Shortly after he met Sils he'd moved from Albany to Horsehearts to be near her. He worked highway construction, and the highway construction, too, had moved north. In the moist cool green of the early mornings, the humidity just beginning to catch the sun and promise heat, she would unstraddle his Harley, out in front of Storyland, when he dropped her off for work, and one could see her attempt to make the shift into day, into light, a Cinderella in reverse. She had a habit, when someone else was around watching, of raising her eyebrows and pointing at him when he spoke, and then in the nick of time returning her face to normal when he looked over at her. Or not. Sometimes he caught the edge of it, a wild bird that had disappeared down her throat, that she had madly swallowed to spare him, and he would stare at her.

"What?" he'd say. This was a demand for an explanation.

"Yeah, what: What do you mean, 'What?' " She would then look to me, or whomever, for an audience, and smile. It was a sweet smile, and almost always resulted in her kissing him afterward. Nuzzling a little. She was a high school girl and this was the first sex she'd known. It drugged her with secrets. It had stolen her away, left her smile deranged, her hair a mess.

"How you doing today?" I asked, petting one of her shoulder blades on the way into the employees' entrance.

"You still wanna go to the Sands tonight, I hope," she said. The Sands was a divey shack on the lake, a tavern called Sans Souci, which had gotten corrupted by the local accent into "the Sands," as if it were some Las Vegas nightclub. We had been going since the previous summer. We could get into all the bars. Though we were minors, we had working papers and hitchhikers' thumbs and the fake IDs we'd made at the library, which had the only photocopy machine in town. We'd borrowed one of Sils's brother's driver's licenses, photocopied it, then retraced our copies, substituting our own photos and names. We did not think of any of this as a crime. Crimes weren't crimes; laws weren't really real; nothing applied. Nothing applied to us. We were set apart by adolescence and geography; the country was in upheaval, there was Vietnam and draft dodging and rock music and people setting themselves on fire. Laws seemed to be the enemy. So we dispensed and dispatched, ceased and desisted: we made up our own rules, and they were loose. We were inventing things, starting over, nothing was wrong. *Tin soldiers and Nixon coming.* Everything was a ticket out; everything was merging, proceeding, leaving home—all the different forms this took. Love. Peace. *Smile on your brother everybody get together.*

And we were the sensible girls. We were known as such. We baby-sat. We scored high on Iowa Tests. No matter that sometimes at night we were at the railroad tracks, drunk on 7-Up and whiskey. That we enticed each other out to dance bars by holding the phone next to a stereo playing Deep Purple or Maggie Bell or Grand Funk Railroad until the other said, "OK, OK, let's go!" The truly wild kids had already left for the pipeline in Alaska or for Boston or Broadway or the med units of Da Nang.

"Oh, yeah. Let's go," I said. She had the next day off.

"Oh, good," she said. "I feel like I never see you anymore."

Later, as an adult, when I was wonderfully used to long, important conversations in restaurants or bars—books, love, politics, science—talk that licked about like a flame, talk that traveled like roads into the night, guided, or urged, I suppose, by drink and hunger, or some chaos of the heart, it seemed to me strange that I had ever enjoyed spending those nights at the Sans Souci with Sils, because I don't recall what we ever talked about. I don't think we had real conversation. We were guitarless, without our music books, we couldn't sing. But we didn't really talk, either. We drank and bantered and remarked and gazed around and once in a while when the music got too loud we shouted something at each other and laughed. We smoked cigarettes, the strange brazen dare of it never abating for us, even though it was only one of so many dares we made, over and over. We ordered gin and tonics and held each one up to the black lights on the ceiling to marvel at the spooky blue and then to drink it. We had no idea what life had in store for us; not a clue, not a thoughtful thought. Inevitably a guy—older, drunker—came over to try to pick up Sils. Almost sixteen, she was the sort of fifteen-year-old who looked twenty. I, to my own shame and uncertainty with the bouncer, was the sort who looked twelve.

"How yew girls doin'?" was inevitably how it began, and then usually the guy fussed with the front lock of Sils's hair, pulling it out of her eyes, or he sat next to her, hip to hip, or he asked what she was drinking or did she want to dance to this song, it was a good song for dancing, it was a good night for dancing, didn't she think so?

Usually it was a humid night, the boards of the place dank as a river dock. Sometimes I protected her with gruffness or a smirk or a cryptic look to make the guy think we were making fun of him. That he was too old. "It's only teenage wasteland," wailed the jukebox during the band's breaks. I would nudge her.

But sometimes I got up and went to the bathroom, let her deal with him, and sometimes later he would give us a ride home at eleven-thirty, hoping for her, dreaming, waiting for us at the corner while we went to one or the other of our houses, said good night to our mothers, went to our room, stuffed pillows under the covers, making curved and lumpy bodies, then climbed out the window.

They didn't seem to mind, these men. I swear: often they just didn't seem to mind. They were half in love already; they were wishing. They wanted servitude to Sils, to get close to her, the prettiness, the breasts, the elegant neck, the long hair fragrant with a girl's shampoo. We'd dash back to the corner to meet up, and the guy would still be there and we'd climb in, Sils in the front, I in the back, and we'd head up to the lake again and I'd watch the guy's right arm go slowly up, stealing up behind Sils on the car seat, making its way around her, a cheap stole, and I'd pray there wasn't a gun. I was a Baptist and had always prayed, in a damp squint, for things not to happen. Sils was a Catholic, and so she prayed for things *to* happen, for things to come true. She prayed for love here and now. I prayed for no guns. Once, the year before, there had been a gun, a pistol fetched from the guy's left boot and waved at us in a wobbly way with his right hand. Our hearts beating and the doors unlocked, when he stopped at a Stop sign, we pushed open the car doors and flew out.

Here he was, a man with spurs and a cowboy hat, wildly pointing a gun at two fourteen-year-old girls, yet stopping, carefully, at all the Stop signs. And so we leaped out and made a dash for it along the road, into some trees, but he got out too, leaving the car running, and chased us with a flashlight, firing his gun once into the air.

Sils froze. I stopped and saw her standing there and so went back, and he burst upon us, crashing through the underbrush, waving the gun. He backed us up against a row of pines and shouted at us to take off our clothes. Sils started to, so then I did too, what else could we have done? I stripped to nothing and stood there in the woods, bare feet on the pine needles and bony roots, one hand behind me clutching the branch of a buckthorn bush, the night sky an eerie, muggy slate, not as dark as it should have been because the moon, though fuzzy from rain, was full as a coin. He looked at me first, shining the light up from my feet, along my scrawny legs and hips and chest to my face and then he laughed coarse and bemused and moved away to flash on Sils, starting from her face, moving down along her shoulders and woman's breasts and girl's tight stomach and legs. "That's right," he said, moving toward her, and then he put the gun down, "that's right," and in the light of the flashlight he still awkwardly held, the beam zigging and zagging, he began to take off his own clothes, not just his pants and spurred boots, but his shirt and his watch and hat, and that's when I looked at Sils and cried out, and then we both twisted and ran, bolted, naked, tearing our already tough feet, bruising the arches on stones, going fast and blind the three miles it took to get us through the woods, making our way toward one group of trees and then another and another, until we were out the other side, over the new highway overpass and down the Bay Road to Dix, then home, back in through the window before dawn. We sank down, catching our breaths. We lay in bed, next to the pillow bodies, not knowing what we felt; we reminisced our lost outfits.

No dude-ranching man ever got hold of us like that again. We were more careful from then on. We studied the eyes, and the backseats, to make sure there wasn't anything strange in them. We were fools, but we wanted things: summer, night, drink, air on our arms, the swell of music, the achy swell of music, or the quiet of the lake roads with no cars, past the parking lot, asters and seeding grass on the side, and us walking, smoking joints, letting the smoke burn and prick our lungs, our legs languid, our eyes stained calm, our legs in a matched pace before we turned and went back inside to dance. Conspirators. Emotional business partners. That's what we were.

Years before, when we were eleven, we'd already begun our myriad personal rituals of assertion and disguise. We'd pretend we were teenagers, put on our "baby doll" dresses, a style briefly popular in the sixties: puffy sleeves and epaulets through which you could thread the chain of a color-coordinated change purse. We'd smear our lips with Yardley lip gloss, plastic pots of strange, sticky pink, which we applied and devoured and which would probably later cause an array of small, inoperable tumors, but from early on it was what we required. Applying thick, distracting tints to my lips was a habit I retained into adulthood, though sloppily, headed for a middle age of hasty, shiny red leaking outside the lines of my mouth, like modern art only scary. As early as sixth grade my teacher had pulled me aside and said, "Benoîte-Marie, what are you wearing on your lips?"

"Nothing," I replied, my first lie to an institutional figure, but I'd felt cornered.

She looked all around my face. She looked at my earrings, which were silver cake decorations I'd glued on with Elmer's.

One of the candies had fallen off in recess and now I had a big scab of glue on my ear. I reached up and picked at it.

"Are you wearing one color on your top lip and a different one on your bottom?" she asked, incredulous.

I was. I thought it looked better that way. Why did she have to be so harsh, with her widow's eagle eye? I had once brought her lilacs, and she'd sent me straight to the principal's office. She knew they were from a neighbor's bush and not my own. Our yard had no lilacs.

"You don't need that stuff," she said. "You're too young."

"What stuff?" I said, and she sighed and let me go. (Decades later, in my one lone year of Housewife's Bathrobe Disease, my husband at work but not me, I would roam through the house, still in slippers and a robe, my face unwashed, my hair unbrushed, but I'd put on lipstick, a bright Indian Red or Scarlett O'Hara, and schluff through the house like that, sort through papers, vacuum.) Our mothers let us do this—wear makeup, and stockings and garter belts, and go off—because they had other concerns. Sils's mother had a job and sons in a rock band. Mine was at a meeting or church or some information fair for foreign students, and at home, when she wasn't mimeographing committee memos from a metal box of brownish jelly heated on the stove (pages and pages of purple lettering produced this way from a single typed sheet), she was chatting with Mrs. LeBlanc, or curled on the couch beneath a raincoat, napping off a depression. Sils and I would go downstreet and lurk. Look for "cute guys," we said. Though when we actually came upon a band of them, my heart always sank.

But it was those times mostly that bonded me to Sils, and made me able later to spot the slightest thought working its way across her face, like a bit of weather, and that is how I knew that morning, my mother dropping me off in front of

Storyland, and me glimpsing Sils arriving at the same time with Mike, and slipping bowlegged off his bike and scraping her ankle on the hot exhaust pipe, a loss of agility peculiar for her, that she was pregnant. It was the spaciness of her worry, the slight separation both from Mike and from me, whom she seemed to try to reach via quick bolts of light and dark she threw into her eyes and then yanked away, put in storage, her eyes becoming a snowman's coal. She'd throw, yank, turn away in loneliness. At home in her room she played E-minor 7 to A-major, over and over on her guitar, saying nothing. Then she'd look at me as if I'd only just arrived and say, *"What?"*

She wasn't telling me, because she thought I was a child. A child with a cottage cheese sandwich. That's what I believed she thought. I was sure.

And so that is why, when she finally did tell me, days later—"I can't believe this, Berie, but I may be pregnant"— I leaped like a hired hand to respond.

"I'll help you," I said.

Though some part of me also hung back, shocked and disbelieving, unable to proceed through the moment, the information. No matter that you anticipate a thing; you get so used to it as part of the future that its actuality, its arrival, its force and presence, startles you, takes you by surprise, as would a ghost suddenly appearing in the room wearing familiar perfume and boots. We were in the Storyland employees' lounge, getting dressed, she as Cinderella, me as my usual striped goof in a pinafore and hat.

"It might not be true," she said. "I feel so bloated. I feel like I'm going to get my period any day now."

"That's one of the signs," I said knowledgeably. I read all the books, fascinated with gynecology the way an android might be.

"When Chrissy Messita was pregnant she had to go to Vermont."

"I'll drive you," I said. I only had my learner's permit, but I was getting good.

"I suppose I can get Mike to drive. But thanks."

I was quiet, thinking about her and Mike Suprenante and what their baby might look like.

"What car would you get, anyway?" she asked.

"What?"

"Whose car would you be able to g—"

"My parents'," I said quickly. I was too young myself for a driver's license, but I thought what I could do was get LaRoue to drive us. "I could wait and catch them on a nice day, when they walk everywhere anyway and wouldn't miss the car."

"I don't think it works like that," she said. She leaned over and placed her breasts in the bodice of the dress, cakes in a cup, and then she turned around for me to zipper her. "You have to make an appointment and go when the appointment is."

It was then that I realized she meant the abortion clinic, not the unwed mothers' home. Last year two pregnant girls we knew from school—Mary Mills and Sara Hayward—had gone to the home to live for four months to have their babies, and Mary Mills, afterward, had serrated her arms with a grapefruit spoon. Abortion was newly legal in the state, but in our county no doctor would perform one; you had to go to Vermont.

"Oh," I said, "that's right." The tinny calliope music started up in the park, and I grabbed my cashier's box, the one with the money and the thick roll of orange tickets, and headed for register three upstairs, to empty the box into the drawer.

"Tonight," Sils called after me. "Don't forget."

"Okey dokes, artichokes." I actually said that. When I was fifteen I actually said that a lot.

I phoned my mother late in the afternoon to say I wouldn't be home for dinner; I got LaRoue instead. She was working at a kennel that summer, cleaning dog cages, and grooming cats, which no one there liked to do except her. "I don't know," she said in her strange proprietary way. "I don't know. Mom won't be too pleased." *Mom.* She always called her that. Now *I* grew strange and proprietary. "She'll live," I said and hung up. I didn't think about LaRoue, who she was, what she might have wanted in her life or from me, who was not exactly in it, but dancing along at the edge like a bean. I acted fidgety with her, jumpy and busy.

I was focused on Sils. That night after work we walked to Dairy Dreem for cheeseburgers and milk shakes, sitting outside across from the old Fond du Lac Fort, taken by the British from the French in the 1700s, and recently reconstructed for the tourists. Once in a while a fake cannon went off, and a teenager dressed in eighteenth-century British military garb—red coat, black hat, ponytail wig—would bang a drum, his summer job. The *Old Paddle Wheel* at the marina would whistle off its steam, and set sail on its dinner cruise. Cars would drive slowly on Route 9, looking for something to happen, or else they would rush, on their way to the beach, or to miniature golf, or to spin painting, or beyond to Montreal. Sils and I sat at Dairy Dreem, at the picnic tables, near the trash cans, eating our cheeseburgers and french fries in wax paper and red plastic baskets. We stirred our milk shakes with long, plastic iced tea spoons. We felt anonymous, Alone Together, like the song; we knew every song there ever was.

"I'm probably stalling," she said, "kidding myself."

I nodded sympathetically, poured more catsup on the wax paper, like some inadvertent symbol, then quickly mopped it up with my fries. I suddenly felt strange. "How long"—and here I cleared my throat—"how long are you overdue?" I sounded like an embarrassed boy, or a nurse. An embarrassed boy-nurse.

I thought she would say a week. Instead she said, "Two months."

"Oh," I said quietly. My grasp of basic syntax palsied. "Shouldn't you try and better hurry soon?"

Sils let her head fall into one palm. Her hair fell in long lines across her face. "God, I feel sick." She shoved her food away. "My problem is I guess I just don't want Mike to know."

I didn't say anything.

"All those years at St. Alphonse's Academy in Albany," she said. "He'll want to keep it. He'll want to get married. I just can't."

"You're too young," said I, the agreeable sidekick, the Greek chorus of one earnest pip-squeak, though the words were those of my sixth-grade teacher, scolding my lipstick; I'd inadvertently seized them, applied them beyond the lines of my mouth.

Sils straightened and looked me square in the eye. She was wearing a rhinestone earring and it caught the setting sun—it did!—sending out a flash of light, like a rescue flare. "How can I not tell Mike and also come up with the five hundred dollars?" We earned a dollar sixty-five an hour. It was 1972, and that was minimum wage.

"I'll get it," I blurted.

"Pardon?"

"The money. I'll get it for you." It was such a daring and

preposterous remark that it silenced both of us, silenced us deep into the evening, even when we were at the Sands, dancing and drinking and bringing on the blur, farming the fuzzy foam, the dream edges, feeling our own watery gait and the tough, hard drums of the band, the ride home perhaps from someone we knew this time; I think it was someone we knew.

And when I awoke the next day, too little, too young for the headache and dry nausea I inevitably had, and too old suddenly with information, the sun cutting through the moist morning already, getting down to business, like a street sweeper, my best friend meditating her abortion, my mother, menopausal and preoccupied, driving me to work and saying nothing, not really, just dropping me off, then adding, "That's sixty-five cents each way, don't forget," so as not to feel used by her children, imposing a lesson about money, how you must pay for everything, nothing is free ("Yes," I said), charging me daily for the lift to work, a practice that now in memory embarrasses me for both of us; why did we live like that, with all that mean, incessant tallying? And me changing from my clothes into my striped dress and pinafore, having learned furtiveness first here, in hiding my too-thin girl's body from the others, looking up my number on the chart, picking up my money box and sorting it out in the drawer of my register—tens, fives, ones, quarters, dimes, nickels, all with their own compartments, fitted together in the square of the drawer like a Mondrian or spice cupboard, and no pennies, just a big blank space for twenties; fifties and traveler's checks under the drawer; it was then I knew what I would do. Of course. I had all A's in math at school; that's why I'd been hired. It came to me in an obvious way, like a chambermaid who year after year sees plane tickets on the nightstands of the rooms she dusts, the rooms of the toilets she cleans, and to whom it comes in a snap, a quick vision, like a stroke of genius or perhaps just a stroke, that she must travel, fly: take these and go. And so she does without a word.

Of course, she is caught.

But I had it planned differently. What I could do, I could do during lunch, when the other cashiers, Sheryl or Debbie, were on their breaks and I had to both ring up and tear the tickets myself, at the perforation, and hand them back to the customers. Customers who were always right.

"The customer always sucks," Sils once said. "Now that's a great motto for an amusement park."

"That's twelve dollars, please."

"But the kid's under four."

"Yeah, right." I'd roll my eyes, and put one hand on my hip.

"What are you, the owner's daughter?" they'd ask.

The children were always indignant. "Daddy?"

"What?"

"I'm *six.* I'm *six.*"

"The kid's not six. Don't listen to him."

"OK. All right. Eight dollars. Here's your tickets. Jesus Christ."

Sometimes I didn't ring up. When the other girls were on break, I pressed the No Sale key, rang open the drawer and sold stubs, keeping track on a scratch pad so that later, before closing, I could reclaim this amount from the register, or sneak it from the money box, which I would take to the bathroom with me, "for extra security."

"That's twenty-four dollars. Here are your tickets."

"That's it? That's all there is to it?" the park visitors ("Visitors to the Park," according to the P.A. system) would say.

"Yup." I would stare straight ahead.

"That's all we get? We just show these?"

"Uh-huh."

"Oh. OK." And they would wander off through the gate into the park.

At first there was never an overage, or a shortage, or a discrepancy of any sort. I would walk across the park with my money box to a snack stand, buy a root beer, and then, heart briefly pounding, go to the bathroom and take out the calculated sum—forty-eight dollars, say, or once, ninety-six—and return the rest to Isabelle, our supervisor, in the office upstairs. It wasn't that scary to do this, for some reason, because—unlike the time I ran under a truck stopped for a red light, rather than walk all the way around it, and unlike the time I hitchhiked alone at night to the lake just to test myself, to learn the *meaning of myself* good god whatever that was, and unlike the time I shoplifted from a downstreet store a sweater I had coveted grossly, in a heat ("hocked," we said; "I like your shirt; did you *hock* it?")—I was doing this for Sils and her emergency.

I kept the money under my stack of records at home—Carole King, Joni Mitchell, Bread—and at the end of the week I had five hundred and fifty-two dollars, pressed flat as envelopes from the weight of all that music.

Sometimes with Daniel I argue about the sixties. He is nine years older than I am, and knows that time better than I, or differently.

"There's a real age difference between us," he says.

"Age-schmage," I reply.

"Unfortunately, there's also a real schmage difference. We made the sixties," he says, speaking in a generational "we" that excludes me. "We made the counterculture. You were twelve years old."

"But we inherited it," I say, "and as children we made ourselves around it, with it. We hung our own incipience on politics. The counterculture got on the ground floor with us, as children; it was the wood we were built with. We used to watch you guys, the eighteen- and nineteen-year-olds, on LSD at the public beach, or playing Duck, Duck, Goose in Horsehearts Park with your beads and long-flowing Indian smocks. But then *we* got to be that age, and we went to the park, or to the lake, and there wasn't a Duck or a Goose or a hit of acid anywhere. There was only Ford pardoning Nixon."

"Christ," snorts Daniel.

"But once upon a time it had been all we knew," I say. "Rebellion, revolution, and all those songs that went with them. We ice-skated to 'Eve of Destruction.' 'The western world, it is exploding,' and we'd do these little spins and turns."

Or something like that. I say something like that.

"But still it was *ours*," he says. "It came from inside of *us*, not you."

"Yes, you made it, but as a result it was a thing outside of you. You could walk away from it. And you did. We couldn't, you see. It was in us. And when it was no longer out there in the world itself, it left us stranded, confused, betrayed, masturbating and doomed little outlaws."

"Masturbating and doomed little outlaws?"

"Sure."

"What are you talking about? You can't use the sixties like this. You can't use the sixties to explain yourself to yourself."

Of course that's what I want. I think of the lies and theft

that cultivate the provincial heart. I had been beyond *questioning* authority. I'd felt unseen by it. But now, looking back, I want to fudge and say it was the *time*, not the place. "But which is more powerful, what you make or what you inherit? Which is more permanent?" I ask. "I realize that we're talking ridiculous generalities here, but let's face it, a discussion is always more fun that way."

"It's a sign," he says, "of a person looking for excuses. A hoodlum seeking politics."

"Perhaps a hoodlum is already politics."

"You're no hoodlum."

"That's true," I say, sighing. And in this lie I feel close to him, so grateful to him, so full of pity.

It goes like that. Our talk goes something like that.

It was on a Tuesday, my day off, that I planned to show Sils the money. I cleaned my room. I vacuumed the purple shag carpet, put new Scotch tape on the back of my *Desiderata* poster so it didn't billow or droop. *Be yourself. . . . You are a child of the universe. . . . Be cheerful. Strive to be happy.* "Where's the part that says, 'Don't run with scissors in your mouth'?" Claude once asked, studying it. The previous school year I'd also taped up a *Let It Be* poster, a Spiro Agnew poster (on which I'd inanely scrawled, in eyeliner, "Yeah, right, Spiro Baby!"), and a psychedelic poster that said, in flame-glo, swirling script, "Life Is a Gas at 39 Cents a Gallon." But this summer I had taken them down and left only the *Desiderata.* Now I dusted the shelves and the dressing table with its loosening, fake-wood contact-paper top and its skirt assembled from an old dyed curtain and some tacks. I had a row of colognes from the drugstore downtown: Eau de Lemon, Eau de Love, Oh! de London (Odekerk! Dad, Odekerk!). I had a small stack of articles from *Seventeen*, articles that advised you how to prepare for a date in one hour, in fifteen minutes, in five minutes, in thirty seconds. (He's striding unexpectedly up the walk! What should you do? *Quick! Brush your hair and tie a freshly ironed kerchief around it!*) I had an electric makeup mirror with three settings: Day–Evening–Office. The Office setting was greenish and particularly lurid, and now I leaned into it, hunting in the wilds of the looking glass, examining my skin, not good, not bad, scouting for swellings and clogs and squeezing where I could the watery flan from my pores. Then I swabbed them red and pure with rubbing alcohol. I put on makeup in a large, theatrical way—dark and bright—as if my face were meant to be seen at a great distance.

I set my hair on mist rollers plugged in under the vanity. I put on a scoopneck leotard and my Wrangler shorts, which I had unhemmed the bottoms of in March and carefully combed to form a fringe of paler blue. I looped my macramé belt through the belt loops. I put on some records, Laura Nyro, Carole King, *my life has been a tapestry of rich and royal hue.* I dabbed vanilla extract and Jean Naté Friction pour le Bain on separate wrists, then rubbed them together, my own particular mix. I wanted to be original. I wanted to be *me!* I removed the rollers and brushed the bobby-pin ridges out of my hair. I fell down on my bed and waited. Actually it was only a mattress, frameless on the floor like Sils's, which is how I wanted it, and I had covered it with a bright orange and pink Indian print spread, a "tapestry," we called them, which I had bought at the Macy's mall in Albany the year before with my mother. "Are you sure you want that?" she had asked.

"I'm sure," I said.

"Well, it's your room." The Albany mall was an amazing, bursting palace to me, and I bought badly there, tastelessly, my head dizzy.

I lay on my bed and looked up. I had a pink floodlight in lieu of the regular ceiling fixture and I had affixed a paper beehive-shaped shade to it; probably a fire hazard. What did I care? I owned nothing of value. Everything would turn out fine. Or else—hell—it would burn. I only wanted my body to bloom and bleed and be loved. I was raw with want, but in part it was a simple want, one made for easy satisfaction, quick drama, deep life: I wanted to go places and do things with Sils. So what if the house burned down.

I heard her bicycle crunch up the driveway then stop. She scratched at the screen with a key, and I got up and went to the window.

"Hi," she smiled, looking up into the house through the rusty grid of our screens. She was wearing her best blue jeans, and her white sleeveless shirt under a jean jacket. I knew her clothes by heart.

"Come on in the front," I said. "The door's unlocked."

"Your parents home?"

"Ehm . . . just LaRoue and my mother."

"Brought along a little something," she said, patting the breast pocket of her jacket. "Leave open the windows of your life, babe." I watched her wheel her bike off to the front and waited to hear the doorbell ring. LaRoue answered.

"Berie," LaRoue shouted gruffly, perhaps even angrily, but why? I never asked. "It's for you. Silsby Chaussée's at the door."

"Let her in," I shouted back.

"You," replied LaRoue, who pounded off to her own room.

"Girls, stop yelling!" called my mother from upstairs.

I met Sils halfway, in the dining room, already coming in, and I grabbed her jacket cuff, turned, and led her back into my room.

"Typical afternoon at the Carr house," said Sils.

"I hate this family," I said, and closed and locked the door. We had old doors in our house: keyholes with skeleton keys we were required to leave in the hole.

Still, I turned the key, locked the bolt in place, and once the door was shut I watched Sils's smile dissolve to a mumble and a stare. "Fuck," she said, fumbling for the joint in her pocket and lighting it with Sans Souci matches. She inhaled and held the smoke deep inside, like the worst secret in the world, and then let it burst from her in a cry.

"Here." She thrust the joint at me and I headed for the back window with it, on my rug-burned knees before the screen, blowing out the smoke.

"I keep thinking about what's inside me," Sils said. "The beginning little Tinkertoys of a kid. But I don't feel anything."

I turned to look at her, but we were sitting too close, so I turned my head back toward the window, looked toward the middle distance, then farther, looked out past the trees, at and through the leaves, and I again remembered that night last year, the one with the man and the gun springing up like a jack-in-the-box, the light summer midnight just beyond and past the branches. We had run, always heading for the next group of trees, and then for the next and then the next, like an enactment of all of life.

"I don't know how I'm ever going to deal with all this without everyone finding out," said Sils.

Everything was getting funny and vague. My records in a pile on the spindle plopped down one by one: the Moody Blues; Stevie Wonder; Billie Holiday; Crosby, Stills and Nash; the Rolling Stones. Every song had the word "Tuesday" in it. "Tuesday Afternoon." "Tuesday Heartbreak." "Ruby Tuesday." *Maybe Tuesday will be my good news day. Will you come see me Tuesdays and Saturdays?*

Maybe it was Thursday and Saturday. But I preferred Tuesday. A day of twos. Sometimes when I sang alone, sprawled rapturously on my bed, the windows open and the cheeping summer night outside in big warm rectangles, calling, calling, I just made the words be whatever I wanted.

"I have something to show you," I said, getting up and handing the joint back to her. I walked over to my record shelf and lifted up my stack of records, the dozens not yet piled on the stereo—Big Brother and the Holding Company, Melanie, Seals and Crofts, a collection of Neil Young concerts lap-recorded by a bootlegger with a cough—and showed her the money, flat and dead, priceless and chloroformed like a flock of butterflies.

Sils stared.

"This is for us," I whispered. "This is all for you."

"The money?" She wasn't comprehending.

I checked the door again. I closed the window and the shades and then sat at my dressing table on the spinning, plush-covered, vanity stool. I turned on the makeup mirror for light. I turned it to Office, its sickly green, and laughed in a cackly way, though I didn't mean to. "I took it," I said.

"You took it?"

"I collected it. I kind of—hocked it. I just, I sold stubs and didn't ring up."

She looked at me and then at the money for a long time. A pumpkin into a coach: I hoped that was what she would see. For today, Tuesday, I would be her fairy godmother. I tried to swallow, but the pot had made my throat bitter and dry, my gums drained and astringed. I had to concentrate not to giggle. Or weep. Or sing. I had to concentrate to see.

At long last she looked up at me. "Don't they count the stubs?" was all she said.

"Nope," I said. "Not that I know of." And then we did laugh. We laughed the laugh of idiots.

Sils fell into an ironic squawk. "This is going to go on your permanent record, missy," she said, shaking her finger.

"We make a dollar sixty-five an hour. Do you think Frank Morenton, who owns half this country anyway, do you think he'd ever notice? He's too busy opening Santa's Little Village up in Dalesburg."

"I suppose it serves him right for not giving us a raise." And now she actually reached toward the money to touch it. "Let's go to the James Gang concert," she said suddenly. Now she was holding up bills. She plucked up a twenty and waved it around.

"Pardon me?"

"The James Gang's giving an outdoor concert at the arts center at the lake," said Sils. "God, with this money, we could take a cab."

"Maybe I can get LaRoue to drive us," I said uncertainly. I wanted to save the money. "Let me go see."

LaRoue was in the kitchen polishing her riding boots. "We're thinking of going to a concert," I said, trying to be kind, lingering, swaying, hinting.

"And you want me to give you a ride." She looked disgusted but also a little sad.

"You want to go with us?" I asked brightly, fakely.

She looked at her riding boots a long time, as if this were a challenge. The boots were set smack on the kitchen table, on a page of the *Horsehearts Gazette.* "What concert is it?"

"It's the James Gang," I said.

"What time?"

God, she was really going to do it. "At eight. But we want to get there by seven."

"What about dinner?"

"It's get-your-own night, Mom said." Every so often my mother refused to cook, calling it, with a festive flair, "get-your-own" night, or "fix-your-own." One year, in one of her darker huffs, she canceled Christmas and called it "Christmas Is Canceled Day."

"Yeah, but I was going to make some brownies and macaroni," said LaRoue. She was hugely overweight, though not even as much as she would be later in life. I blinked.

"Don't do that," I said. "Come with us. We can stop at Carroll's." Carroll's was a fast-food shack that would soon be put out of business by McDonald's. But at the time, we liked Carroll's best, the bright red and turquoise colors, the squared and streamlined script of the name.

"OK!" she said. And as she said it, I realized again that I never did anything with LaRoue because she was odd and friendless and I was embarrassed by her, in a way that made me feel bad, but in a way that was sad and unshakable.

I sat in the front seat and Sils in the back, and I kept turning around and all the way up to the lake we kept singing "And When I Die," in the harmony parts we had learned in Girls' Choir the past year. Our choir director, Miss Field, had worked up a nice arrangement of it.

"'I'm not scared of dyin' and I don't really care,'" began Sils.

"'If it's peace you find in dying, well then let the time be near.'"

"'All I ask of livin' is to have no chains on me!'" We practically shouted it. We were best on that line, taking it loud but slow, with some odd intervals, though most of them thirds. We actually didn't know any songs by the James

Gang, or we knew one, the famous one, the one that was a hit, but we didn't know it very well.

At Carroll's we ordered hamburgers and vanilla milk shakes and sat inside at the Formica counter, watching each other eat, or else watching some guy sweep behind the fryer or some guy pull up outside with his car eight-track blaring "In-A-Gadda-Da-Vida" or LaRoue, watching us, like we were up to something.

The parking lot at the Lake Arts Center was already full, and attendants were routing people into a spare one in the rear, usually reserved for employees. We parked there, got out, and headed for the entrance, an old blanket over our arm, a six-pack of Coca-Cola, and a pack of cigarettes. All around us were young men in beards and cutoffs, women in peasant dresses, buffalo sandals, and silver bracelets, carting thermoses, ice chests, lawn umbrellas that said "Peace." Police were stationed just inside the entrance to inspect thermoses and ice chests for alcohol, but besides that there was something wonderful in the air: the loud, crowded, summery feeling of a rock concert, not Woodstock maybe, but we had only been twelve then. This was something festive for us now that we were fifteen; everyone older had been doing this for a while, and they did it with calm and know-how; nothing new or disorganized. Some of them carried babies. We observed them, fell in close to them in line, sat next to them on the lawn. Lawn seats were the cheapest: two-fifty apiece. We paid, got our tickets, headed in.

Music, for us back then, evoked various exiling and confounded moods, states of hallucination, states of love. A song was the timeless truth beneath the surface of things. It was a standing-still trip to the sea! It was a blow to the chest, like a boy you liked suddenly entering the room. It filled you with excitement and shy, deep knowledge. Two-fifty was nothing. We pushed ahead, fell in with the pace of the crowd. We prepared our hearts for something drenching and big.

Somehow we got separated from LaRoue. Did we intend to? I remembered a stinginess of hers in the car, how she'd refused us the chewing gum she had four sticks of in her pocket, and as Sils and I moved through the gate, past the ticket takers and off at a slight diagonal, the crowd moved in between LaRoue and us. She was trudging too slowly behind. I thought I heard her voice, but I didn't turn around.

"Hey, you guys. Wait up!"

We kept walking straight for a favorite place on a hill near a concrete piling, the place we usually sat at concerts, leaning up against the cement to drink our Cokes, moving in under the balcony ramp in case it began to drizzle.

"Where's LaRoue?" asked Sils.

I finally turned around. I couldn't see her anywhere. And the success of this treachery, of my having used her so completely, stunned me. Where was she? Now I scanned the curving bowl of the concert lawn full of faces and heads and blankets and jackets and ice boxes, and I thought perhaps I did see LaRoue way off to one side, on some dirt, sitting alone without a blanket, looking lost and fat.

"I don't know where she is," I said. "We'll get a ride back some other way." I said this breezily. "We'll hitch."

"Maybe," said Sils cautiously. "I wish I'd brought a joint." She lit a Salem instead, and offered one to me, which I took.

Linda Ronstadt opened for the James Gang and everyone talked all the way through it, as if she were just some local girl who'd managed to crawl up there and fill time. When the James Gang finally appeared the crowd stood and cheered. The sky had darkened, and the stage shone bright as fire in a hearth. Everywhere in the air was the ropy smoke of pot. The boys next to us offered us some of theirs, and we took it, in turn, placing our own mouths where theirs had been on the wet paper, then passing it along, like a communion plate or a petition of ash and saliva: a large, smoking spitball shot out at all the teachers of the world. "Good evening, ladies and gentlemen!" The crowd roared, and the band started up.

For the next hour electric guitars wailed and keened in protest of all that we were forced to be in this life. "Man, oh man," murmured the people around us. Four boys climbed up on the second-tier railing and swayed back and forth to the music, their limbs occasionally jolting and spazzing. It was a dance style I'd seen before. It was acid—something that scared and fascinated me. "Do you want to take a trip, a sugar trip, a trip to sugar mountain?" I'd been asked that before at bars. "No thanks," I'd said. For all my recklessness, I feared chromosome damage. I feared accidentally starting a brand-new species. I believed all the talk about damage to your very *genetic material*—though it turned out later not to be true.

I could have been up there with those boys.

There was a slight snap in the air from the lake, and Sils and I huddled under the blanket for warmth. Feeling the heat of her so close, I thought about how seldom we slept over these days, me in that sleeping bag at the foot of her bed, or she at the foot of mine, the routine intimacy of that, our talking out into the dark of our rooms, the cemetery quiet out the window and us with our jokes and sighs and then our sleep, side by side in duet, our breaths staggered like a round. Only once had we ever had a fight—she accused me of having deliberately developed a laugh like someone else, someone named Leslie Fish. She accused me of wanting to hang out with Leslie and be like Leslie, which summoned up such outrage on my part that I struck Sils in the arm and then rushed home in tears, waiting the week out until at last we were friends again.

It had been true about the laugh, and I never laughed like that again.

Now everyone on the lawn stood and so did we, in our large blanket cape, and the whole audience lit matches for an encore, the ground around us like some fantastic birthday cake in the dark, but the band refused to come back. So we packed up and made our way toward the exit with the crowd. I looked in vain for LaRoue, my cruelty toward her now in me like a splinter, where it would sit for years in my helpless memory, the skin growing around; what else can memory do? It can do nothing: It pretends to eat the shrapnel of your acts, yet it cannot swallow or chew.

I looked toward the lot where we had parked, but the car seemed not to be there.

"Let's call a cab," said Sils.

"What do you mean?"

"With the money," she said. "Let's take a cab back home."

"There's probably someone here we know." I was reluctant to spend the money like this.

"Like who?"

"I don't know. Maybe Markie Russo and those guys," I said. Markie Russo had once had a crush on Sils and I was sure he would have given her a ride home in a second. But everyone was heading purposefully toward their cars and I recognized none of them. We were still walking with the blanket around us, like medieval orphans.

"There's a phone," said Sils, and so we called a cab. Hiller's Cab Company. "I'll be there as soon as possible," said the voice at the other end. We waited right there by the phone booth, smoking cigarettes, tapping our feet, watching the dispersing crowd.

The cabbie who came for us was a strange dwarf of a

man: balding, shiny head; fingers fat as wursts; his body squat and globular; his legs so short and misshapen there was some apparatus constructed on the pedals of the cab so that he could drive.

We got in, gave him my address, and he pulled out of the parking lot. The traffic was heavy from the concert and jammed at the next corner near the main light. In his rearview mirror he could see us sorting our money. We had brought forty dollars with us and were counting what was left.

"Where you girls work?"

I didn't say anything. I looked out the window, past the traffic, toward the lake.

"Storyland," said Sils. There was something brazen and high from the pot in her voice. "I'm Cinderella there," she added. I could tell she wanted, just for the fun of it, to shock him somehow.

"Is that right?" He looked in the rearview mirror again, to check her out, I supposed. But instead he looked mostly at me. As if I were the guard or the interpreter. "I used to work there myself as Humpty Dumpty—before they got that ceramic, mechanical one." Now he turned hopefully to look at us both in the backseat.

"Really?" I said.

"Should we call you Humpty?" asked Sils.

"Sure." He smiled.

"We can't call you Humpty," she chided. "We'll have to call you, um—Humphrey!" and we burst our laughing, in a stoned, mean way, but he laughed with us, and we all just sat there in the night traffic laughing in the uncontrolled, hysterical way of people who rarely got what they wanted in life though they also didn't try very hard.

We didn't stop. The laughter built—especially his—to tears and gasps. Three fools from Horsehearts—how funny! We couldn't stop. Even after our cabbie grew quiet, Sils and I sank against the cab doors and snorted, while he sighed and cleared his throat, silently taking the correct turns and driving us the ten miles back to my house. I thought of the time in fifth grade when our science teacher had made some of us be planets and positioned us in town according to where the planets would actually be, relatively speaking. The downtown library was the sun, and Jerry Murphy, who was Mercury, was positioned right there on the library steps. He was dressed in red and carried a little sign with the name of his planet on it. Sils had been Venus and was made to stand by the Civil War monument, two blocks away, draped in gauzy material meant to resemble clouds. But I was Pluto, and had to stand several miles outside of town, in the middle of the countryside. The teacher drove me there herself. And I stood there all afternoon, in black leotards, next to a dairy farm and a cornfield, with my little sign that said Pluto. The local paper came by and took my picture and Sils's older brothers drove past in their car and honked and hooted. Despite the humiliation, I felt close to Sils then. Because of her brothers. Because we were in outer space together, and her brothers had come by to see me.

Which for some reason was how I felt now in the cab, with the cabbie, and our all laughing together. I felt, perhaps because of the pot, like we were all planets in the same solar system—which was all I had ever wanted or asked from people, anyone, ever.

"Thanks," we said when we got out. And we tipped him twenty dollars, "just to blow his mind," Sils whispered.

"Do you think we did? Do you think we blew his mind?"

He hadn't looked to examine the bills. He'd just stuffed them into his pocket.

"He'll look. He'll see," said Sils.

When we went inside, only Claude was still up. He was

sprawled on the couch, under a blanket, watching TV like a
sick person. In the last six months he'd been growing in the
pale, disproportionate way of adolescents and leggy plants—
his limbs and feet sending themselves out past his cuffs like
antennae. But he was still a little boy and self-conscious. I always suspected him of having a crush on Sils.

"Hi," he grunted, turning his head just slightly to see us,
then he blushed and turned back to the television.

"Hi," I said.

"Hi, Claude," Sils said a little flirtatiously.

"Hi," he said again.

"Did LaRoue already come in?" I asked, suddenly worried.

"Yeah," he said absently. That was all. We tiptoed back
to my room, trying not to squeak the floorboards and bring
one of my parents down to lecture us for staying out late and
being generally inconsiderate what was it with us girls.

When later in life she would appear—in a dream with a
group of people, or in a thought about friends I never saw
anymore, those I'd consented to lose and live without—she
often appeared, in sleep or pensiveness, as she did the next
morning when she awoke, dashed to the bathroom, and
threw up. She came back to the room gray and perspiring,
and I gave her my bathrobe to wear. It was a white seersucker
robe, and her hair fell to the inside of the neck of it, making
a kind of pageboy, a frame, like the hood of a cape around her
face. It was the way she often looked in winter, when she
wore a coat: her hair tucked inside, looking as if it had suddenly been bobbed. I knew all the hairstyles and looks of her;
there were a dozen or so, and I knew them all. Each time I
saw one again, I would say to myself, "Oh, yes, that one."

"I'm going to have to make an appointment and just go,"
she said.

I brought her orange juice and ice water and toast buttered so hard it had ripped the bread.

"I'll go with you," I said. "We'll call Humphrey, and we'll go."

Which is what we did.

The following week Sils went to the local doctor, was given a pregnancy test and a referral. Then we phoned Humphrey, our cabbie, got him to meet us at the rear entrance of Horsehearts Park, near the pond where the heartless horses had reputedly been tossed, and we hopped into our cab to Vermont.

"Glad to see you girls again." The drive was along the old Boston Post Road, and then up through farmland, mountains, past little orchards and churchyards with saintly white churches and graves. It was going to cost seventy-five dollars, round-trip, tip included. I remember thinking that once there had been a time when women died of brain fevers caught from the prick of their hat pins, and that still, after all this time, it was hard being a girl, lugging around these bodies that were never right—wounds that needed fixing, heads that needed hats, corrections, corrections.

"Glad to see you, too," I said.

Now the countryside rolled by us, in a timeless way, and I felt like Robin Hood within it. Rob, pay, give away: however improvised, there was beauty to thievery; there were also rules. But I felt I understood them. I felt the pure priestly rush of their fulfillment swell and shrink and swell again within me.

We had the address of the clinic—217 Elm Street, Rutland—and we had six hundred and fifty dollars in fives and tens, a few twenties. Sils was wearing a shirt of mine—a green floral blouse with puffed shoulders and tiny buttons down the front. For some reason she'd wanted to. She'd stood in front of my closet and pulled it off the hanger. "Can I wear this to my abortion?" she'd asked, and, startled, I said, "Sure, if you want," though the request frightened me and caused me to think too much about blood. I wondered whether I should have said yes at all. But now she sat beside me, wearing it, looking better in it than I ever could, her breasts pushing out at the fabric, whereas mine always shrank and shivered behind the hollow drape of it.

We passed through Hope, Argyle Hall, Mt. Bliss, and East Creek, the site of the East Creek Doll Hospital, where, when I was little, my mother would take my dolls to be repaired, an old Victorian house filled to the rafters with broken dolls— Barbies and baby dolls sitting bright-eyed all on top of one another in the parlor, on the stairs to upstairs, in the casements of the windows. The old woman who lived there collected dolls for their spare parts, eyes and limbs mostly, and if your doll had anything wrong with it, you could bring it to this woman, and she would fix it, keep it overnight. "We'll just keep her overnight and give her some tea and some rest." She was crotchety and doddering but with a magic wink that softened her face so that children could see she wasn't scary; she wanted that known. Many of the grown-ups in town, the ones without daughters, didn't know for sure. Her house seemed a witchy one, with spiders on the porch and a skyload of bats flying from her chimney at dusk.

Now that we were passing the house I wondered whether the woman was still there. Ten years had gone by—how old would she be now? I remembered years before seeing boxes out behind the house, boxes of just arms, or just legs, or just eyes, and I wondered what it would be like to see those boxes now, on this particular errand, from this particular cab. I twisted to see, as the taxi sped past, and could see heads and faces and little dresses in the front window. The house was still white with pink trim; there was still a porch swing, and a wishing well in the yard, but there was now also a gas station and a Qwik Stop next door.

"There's the doll hospital," sighed Sils, "with all its cheap irony." Cheap Irony was the name of her brothers' old band.

"Yeah," I said. I twisted back toward her, to look at her, but she turned quickly away, leaned up against the armrest, and looked out at the hot road.

In those days in Horsehearts nothing, no building, had air-conditioning. After a summer rain, humidity soaked into the wood—the moldings, railings. Windows swelled at the sashes and joints. The steps and banisters went pulpy soft, the varnish gummy, the doors sticky and suddenly trapezoidal. The steamy heat fogged the glass, made every cracker in the house go stale. Earwigs roamed and measured the sinks. The hot tar roofs and rubber-lined gutters filled the air with a damp burnt smell.

But here, in this cab, there was air-conditioning. Things were sharp and clean—a luxury that took all sense of emergency out of what we were doing. It seemed we had won a little prize, and no matter our sadnesses we got to go on our cool, crisp trip. We said very little. Once in a while Humphrey turned on some music—we heard most of "A Horse with No Name"—but the reception wasn't good through the mountains, and so mostly he'd turn the radio off again. Ordinarily, we might have sung in the silence, but I wasn't going to unless Sils did first. I kept looking to see whether she would. "La-la-la-la-la-la," she sang out once in a joky way, and then stopped.

"Loo-loo," I sang. "Lee-lee."

We passed charred old farmhouses, orchards, and cornfields. "We could all do a frog chorus," I suggested loudly. A frog chorus was where each person said the name of a vegetable over and over, everybody doing it at once, at differing pitches, to create an amusing din. *Potato, potato, potato. Carrot, carrot, I don't carrot all.*

Sils gave me a dismal, withering look, one that said, "Don't be pathetic." Then she turned back toward the window.

God, how life was full of moments that should have gone differently but didn't.

"Rutland! We're here!" called out Humphrey. "What's the address again?"

"Elm Street," said Sils quickly, looking a little pale. "Two-seventeen." She had memorized it like a combination to a lock. When the cab pulled up in front, she got out quickly, swung her shepherd's bag purse over her shoulder, and walked fast.

"Wait here," I said to Humphrey, wondering how it felt to be bossed around by two girls.

"Whatever," he said. I handed him thirty-five dollars, then I too got out fast and followed Sils, and my green shirt, to the sign that said Clinic Entrance.

Inside, after Sils signed in, and I handed the nurse all my money (except two twenties for the cab ride back, in the front pocket of my shorts) and the nurse counted it out on the reception desk in front of us, we sat in old brown leather chairs, waiting for Sils's name to be called. I'd brought a deck of cards, and we played honeymoon bridge for at least twenty minutes, me winning, and then Sils winning, and then basically a tie.

"Silsby Anne Chaussée?" read a nurse off a clipboard, though there was no one else in the room.

"Bye," I peeped.

"Bye," Sils squeaked back.

I waited there for a while, reading pamphlets—"Contraception," "Venereal Disease and You"—the heat of the room beading in the philtrum of my lip. Then I headed back outside to sit in the air-conditioned cab with Humphrey.

I climbed into the backseat and slammed the door. The air was icy and startling in a nice way. "Hi," I said. What must he think of us, of what we were doing? He didn't say. He simply stared out the front windshield and occasionally looked into the rearview mirror.

"Thought I'd wait in here," I said.

"That's fine." He shifted in his seat a little.

"Do you want to play honeymoon bridge?" I asked.

He shifted, twisted around slightly, and smiled in a lop-sided, ungainly way. "How's it go?"

I hoped he wasn't going to be perverted. You never knew. "I'll show you," I said in a teacherly way, and I climbed out with my cards and got into the front seat with him, dealt out the hands, and explained.

After ten minutes, he was shifting excitedly in his seat. "I think I'm getting the hang of this," he announced. His short legs thrashed with joy.

"It's a great game," I said, though I was losing, too timid in the bidding.

After about forty-five minutes there was a knock at the window. It was Sils looking hot and annoyed, and I leaped out to greet her. I put my hand on her thin tan upper arm. "Are you OK?"

"Where *were* you?" she asked.

"I came out here where it was cooler."

Humphrey reached around to unlock the back door and we both piled in, Sils a little gingerly, I with a kind of rushed efficiency, still clutching my bridge hand. Humphrey handed me the rest of the pack. "All set? Time to go back?"

"Yeah," I said.

"Can we stop for a Coke somewhere on the way?" Sils asked a little absently.

"Sure," I said.

"No problem," added Humphrey and I simultaneously, like a frog chorus after all.

Through the whole drive back I kept trying to steal glances at Sils to see if she looked any different. She had now gone through so many things that I hadn't, I wondered more than ever whether she could still like me, be the same as she had been, or even remember things we'd done together. Was there a ghost, an amphibious baby ghost, flying out behind us, above us, all the way home like a kite? Under Sils's arms there were dark circles of perspiration on my green shirt. Her hair had grown oily and the front had separated into strands. I leaned over to loosen the buckle of my sandals, and when I turned to look up at her, from that angle, I could see a small, golden bugger floating in the dark of her right nostril like a star—odd and alone, speaking dizzily without words.

We found a drive-in—Custard's Last Stand—five miles past the Vermont state line, and there we all got out for Cokes, all three of us sitting awkwardly on one of the picnic tables outside. We gave Humphrey the money, and he got out of the car, limping from the hip, and fetched the drinks. We had commandeered this round, broken egg of a man— the human omelette!—but he seemed to like it. Back beside us, he sipped his own Coke slowly, expectantly. He looked happily around at us to see what we'd say next, as if we were the source of unending amusement and surprise. The Green Mountains were to the back of us, the Adirondacks to the front, and although the sun set sooner in the mountains, it was still only five o'clock, the very summit of a long summer afternoon, and it wouldn't be dark until nine. Four more hours of sun and heat and this day—which I was starting to experience with the vertigo of the sick, the way the sick fall beneath the slats of each minute, looking up at things from the spaces in between, the world faraway and in stripes of light—would be over. I felt not myself. I felt beneath some-where, in a pool of breath and gas.

I had to work at Storyland that night, the seven-to-ten shift, strange for me, but I was taking over for another cashier who needed the night off for a party, she said, though she'd told Isabelle her aunt had died and she had to go to the wake.

"You girls take care" was all Humphrey said, before he dropped us both off at Storyland, where Mike was waiting to pick up Sils.

"Where've you been?" Mike yelled over his revving Harley, and I saw her weakly, automatically, get on his motorcycle and forget to wave to me until they were halfway down the road and then she looked back and waved.

Inside, Storyland was mobbed with people, but the dressing room was empty, and I changed into my ludicrous uniform in an open, careless way, no longer hiding myself, no longer letting my shirt form a large wreath around my neck to hide my chest but just letting my whole body briefly live in the air of the room as I never really had, in my shame at looking so little. Seeing my reflection in one of the mirrors on the side of a row of lockers I could see how lanky and thin I was, skeletal; there were dark circles under my eyes, bug bites on my sticklike arms, bruises on my shins. But my hair was in a cloud, bushy in the heat, wild and wavy, and it alone caused me to feel that I was starting to bloom, that I was a blossom bursting out the top of myself, through the skull, like an anemone the very heat of whose thoughts caused appendages to sprout searchingly in water: I was no longer just a girl with nothing to think or do. For a moment, be-fore I walked out with my straw hat and uniform and money box to stand mechanically in the muggy night, I was some-thing else.

THERE IS a joke about a middle-aged woman who happens upon a frog in the woods. "Kiss me! Kiss me!" says the frog, "and I'll turn into a handsome prince!"

The woman stares, entranced, but doesn't move.

"What's the matter?" asks the frog, growing impatient. "Don't you want a handsome prince?"

"I'm sorry," says the woman, "but at this point in my life I'm actually more interested in a talking frog."

"I get it," says Daniel. "That's funny. That's good." I take his hand, lay it across my mouth, press it there. In travel one's husband's body becomes yours; you become united, merged, and you have the same arguments with it that you would with your own. Travel, at those times, becomes love, possession, the second wedding—not just an excuse an unhappy person can use to wear the same clothes every day. Which is what it could be, otherwise.

The gurgling coo of pigeons awakens us each morning. "Wake up and eat the daisies," Daniel whispers to me. We watch the pigeons leap winglessly from the ledges, as if in sailor dives, only spreading their wings at the last minute.

"Is that for aerodynamics?" I ask. "Is that to work up momentum?"

"It's laziness," says Daniel. "They're just being lazy."

Here in the Marais we wake early in the mornings and are in bed early at night. We miss National Public Radio. We miss recycling, as silly or meager as that sounds. Everything we use here must be thrown away, and it bothers us, robbed of our rituals of composting and reclamation, our daily treks out back to the rot-heap, where we offer the Earth scraps of itself, returning nature to nature! Expediting the Global Easter, when all shall rise again! Though we mean it, and mean to, we've never actually used the compost: it is merely an act of apology.

While here for three weeks we live in unapologetic sin. Touristic waste, native presumption. The Parisian meanness makes us despair, so grounded in opinion as it is—unlike the meanness of Americans, which is all careless ego, selfishness, the stuff of spoiled, stupid children.

At night, Daniel is tired from the medical conference he is here at the Institut de Génétique to attend. As a researcher he is mostly, recently, interested in the Tay-Sachs gene we both carry—what Jews and French Canadians have in common ("We'll simply tell our daughter we got her retail rather than wholesale," says Daniel, after we investigated the difficult procedures of adoption, the empty room upstairs we call the "Maybe's Room" still empty, our desires becoming courteous, less determined, discerning the hoops and circumstances). Now this conference seems to him bogged down with squabbles about who should be in charge of the institute itself, research ownership, other such infighting. "All the lying and coffee it takes to get anything done at all," he says, have exhausted him. "Quick, a bonbon!" he exclaims.

"Well, you're fighting the good fight," I say.

"I'm crying the good cry." He sighs.

"You're doing fine."

I teach him a version of honeymoon bridge, the same version Sils and I used to occupy ourselves with. We don't keep score, but we each try to win. When he gets a bad hand, he falls forward, sighing, "This hand is a foot!," a line from some dissolute uncle of his. That—along with our Chez Stadium, *mais oui*/may we jokes, and Pépé LePew imitations—somehow keeps us amused, a brief contentment; it is a respite from out petty quarrels and brittle looks, arguing, as tourists do, about where we're going, where we are, the questions no longer just metaphorical but literal, replete with angry pointing and some disgusted grabbing of maps, right out of the other's hands.

By Wednesday morning Daniel decides to go to a *gymnase* club before his meeting. He's up promptly, with the throaty rumble of the pigeons, the sky-whitening sun, the garbage trucks trolling along the curbs, and the Siamese cat on the roof of the neighboring building, the slight honk of baby in its cry, scratching at a window to be let in. Daniel's grown restless and irritable. "This would be a great town," he says at breakfast over *café crème*, "if only everyone spoke Spanish." His voice is full of rue. "Also, why does everyone in the whole city have to touch the bread? You go to buy bread, and the baker touches it, the cashier touches it, the assistant hands it over to you, then finally you yourself just tuck it under your armpit and go out and bump into other people on the street with it. How can we have a medical conference in a town with such unsanitary bread?"

This is not simple, joky Ugly Americana. This is Daniel's way. It is like at home when he complains about emptying the dishwasher: "This is not a time-saving device. Why has no one invented something that will just wash these things right in the cupboard?" It is his habit to locate all the lapses and betrayals of the modern world. Yet it is also his habit to want to believe what he reads. He heads for places with signs that say *On parle anglais ici*. "But *On* is never there. Have you ever noticed that?"

"You're doing fine here," I say. "Think of it this way: the French love Jerry Lewis. They probably *adore* you." The world in italics. "Think of this as a kind of *Doctors in Paris* thing. A musical." But even the italics, it seems, are losing their italics: standing tall, passing themselves off as literal and real. Straight shooters.

He gives me a look, then turns. "I like the weather," he adds enthusiastically. "You need a jacket, but you don't have to zip it!" Then he adds darkly, "It's that Deportation Monument. That tells you who the Parisians really are." The Deportation Memorial, in the shadow of Notre-Dame, is something we stumbled upon two days before and it left us dumbstruck. "And another thing: have you ever noticed what the supreme Parisian compliment is? 'Oh, you speak French so well, without any *accent*!'"

"It's horrible," I agree. "It's rude."

"It's more than rude," he says. "It's genocidal." And he is right, I think. He is right.

With my middling French and leather jacket—unzipped!—trying to seem residential, I go with him to the gym, to get him settled there. We pay the money and I ask the woman at the desk if there is anything else, any rule or requirement. She smiles. She looks at Daniel. "The only requirements is that you be happy man," she says. She is tan from sunlamps and is wearing an orange leotard.

"Bye," I say to him. *"Au revoir."* I leave to make my way alone along the ankle-twisting stones of the smaller crowded streets, my leather jacket squeaking like a chair. Perhaps I should go shopping—a married person's version of dating. Perhaps I should ditch the jacket and float around in the museums like a sylph, or a balloon.

People bump into me, and I say "Whoops" or "Wope"— not words that translate into any Parisian comprehension, though they're the first sounds to my lips. Almost always. With everything.

I go slow, with my hip.

Passing cafés and restaurants, I walk through the bright glance of men in love, who, looking briefly away from the lover across from them in order to more perfectly form a sentence, unwittingly cast their gaze across my path like a light. And so, momentarily, to have accidentally caught their desire, swimming across the current of it like that, passing through, I feel loved, in a warm and random way, wandering through it, as if it were a rainbow, that old trick of light, or a place in a pool where someone has peed. There is a sweet, silent rot to it.

Otherwise, it is hard, galumphing along through a sea of Frenchwomen who have exquisite shoes and haircuts, overbites unruined by orthodontia, faces unbedecked by optometry, a great, nearsighted, chomping faith in their own beauty that makes them perhaps seem prettier than they are. It is hard to find a place for yourself in a city like this.

The trees are like candelabra. The pastries like art.

There is a smell one begins to exude here: something old-mannish and acrid, like our cabbie coming in, something to do with the food, the wines and *chèvres*. My body fights travel, sends up the weapons of a homeless person, the boundaries thinly drawn, the body with its own knowledge, disorientations, defenses: the winy sweat, the cheesy shit. It takes me walking, then sits me down again, over and over, its own rhythms and wants.

My hip still aches from my fall last December, the cracked bone moody and susceptible to weather, but if I need to I limp. Perhaps somewhere I'll just stand against a wall and ask for coins.

"Paris," I hear a passing tourist remark. "It's one big StairMaster."

There is an Audrey Hepburn festival at one of the revival theaters on the Left Bank, and everywhere I see posters for it: Hepburn's wide eyes and mouth. "Have you ever noticed," Daniel has said, "that she looks like Anne Frank?" Now I feel as if I'm seeing pictures of Anne Frank all over town: Anne Frank in a black turtleneck. Anne Frank in an evening gown. The essence of Paris, Daniel might say, there you go: Anne Frank in an evening gown.

The italics are losing their italics.

The flower beds are full of pansies whose triangular, black centers boast the mustache of Hitler himself.

I stop at *pâtisseries* and get the pastries with funny names: Divorce, Religieuse, Gland. I like the Divorce ones—half coffee, half chocolate—and I sit in the Luxembourg Gardens, eating my various Divorces, watching the children throw things into the pond. Planted in large, gorgeous ovals are tulips so big they look as if they'd steal your jewelry. There are school groups here on tour, the girls giddy and tired and falling into one another's laps, playing with one another's hair. The boys stand around looking exiled and sad.

I get up and walk some more, back across the river: the views of the city up and down dazzle and console. Near the Louvre, which is being cleaned, always being cleaned, two angels and some cherubs have been removed, set in locked crates at the edge of the Tuileries and one can walk by and look at them through the slats, see them regally sitting there, a zoo of pagan saints, their winged and caged condition like the aftermath of some palace revolt in Heaven. *Aw*, I find myself thinking. *Aw.*

A lot like *Whoops. Wope. Whoops-a-daisy.*

I go into the Louvre, but I don't stay long. It's too different now. I've lived long enough to see the great museums change: their annexes and entrances, the location and arrangement of the art. My own memory, from a trip ten years ago, is a tired, old coin. Who will house that? Who will house the Museum of Museums, in order to show us how museums once were?

I decide to get on the *métro* and go visit my friend Marguerite, who is a painter and printmaker, half French, half American, with an apartment near the Bois de Vincennes. I phone her from Châtelet. *"Allô, oui?"* she answers, which sounds to my bad ear like *A lui*, to him, to God, some religious utterance, a curse, or something to safeguard the speaker, but she explains later, "Oh, no. It's said that way just in case the caller hasn't heard the *'allô.'* It's a French distrust of technology."

"In a country *farci* with nuclear power plants?"

"Ah, oui," she says. *"Les contradictions."* Marguerite is a woman I met in college, and though we were not that close, we always remained interested in each other and in touch. She is the sort of woman about whom others ask, "Oh, how is she? Is she still beautiful?" She reminded me early on of what perhaps Sils would be, could have been—she is tall and

dazzling like that—and so I bring her my crush, inappropriate but useful between adult women, who need desperately to be liked and amused, and will make great use of any silent ceremony of affection. For the time being Marguerite is on Parisian welfare, which is so civilized as to provide tickets to such French necessities as movies and restaurants, and though she is loath to admit it, she is half-looking for a rich husband. In her I excuse everything I wouldn't like in anyone else.

"I'll be the one in the pith helmet," I say before I hang up, wondering what that even means.

At her *métro* stop I get off and walk the three blocks to where she lives. She is sitting on the curb outside her building, like a kid rather than the forty-year-old woman she is. She has cut her hair off, shaved her head on one side, and with big antique earrings she manages to make all long hair seem a slatternly, inelegant bore. *"Bonjour, mademoiselle!"* I call in greeting, and when I get close, go suddenly formal; I stick my hand out and my fingers lock and go stiff, like a fistful of knives and forks. Luckily, she leaps up and hugs me, does the one kiss on the cheek, then two, three, four. "Four is chic now," she says.

"I need Dramamine for four," I say.

"It's French love!" she says, and takes my arm, steers me through the locked gates and doors.

Inside she offers me water, shows me her work, her serigraphs, her latest culinary effort (*terrine de lapin*: bowl of bunny), and even her new makeup, expensive and Japanese.

"Great," I say loudly, idiotically, to everything. "Great!" She waves the makeup brushes around, the lipsticks and bottles, shouting, "Get out of my way, French women!" Which makes me laugh, because she is so beautiful already and because I have always thought of *her* as French. She points to her short skirt. "I will not cut my fashion to fit this year's conscience."

I smile. She has good legs. "Don't," I advise.

She wants to show me the galleries in her neighborhood, to demonstrate what, in a curatorial culture, "now constitutes the dynamic."

"Great," I say. So we leave the apartment, lock the door, tramp around the neighborhood. We visit an exhibit called "What Else Is There but Narcissism, I Often Ask Myself"—a collection of strangely silvered mirrors. We see another that is simply an arrangement of hundreds of dead pigeons. The artist, the gallery says in its write-up, was a homeless person, and this is his revenge on the pigeons who used to steal bread from his hands. After this installation opened, the gallery brochure informs us reassuringly, the artist received a grant.

"Are you OK?" asks Marguerite, noticing my walk. "You have a tourist's blister? You have one of those *underwear* blisters?"

"It's an old injury from the winter." I begin to lie. "I slipped down the icy stairs at work."

"At the Historical Society?"

"Yes," I say. I cannot tell her the truth. Or can I? *Can I tell you the truth?* I might begin. And she might say, *Bien sûr.* And I would explain that, well, after weeks of fighting and months of door-slamming straight out of the most boisterous of farces, Daniel pushed me down the stairs.

Non, tu blagues! she'd say. And I would continue.

Non, je ne blague pas! Could I tell her? I was at a cocktail party with Daniel at Doctors' Park, where his lab used to be. It always stank at Doctors' Park, some war of septic and antiseptic, and I hated it there. He was flirting with a woman, and the woman's husband turned to me and said in a rambunctious voice, "Well, your husband's number at work is certainly a number at work!" He was drunk and winked at me in a bitter way. Then he began to sing "Every Valley Girl shall be exalted," something meant for his wife to hear. They were going to have a fight when they got home. When Daniel was finished flirting, I went up to him and said, "Let's go. I need to eat."

"Why do you need to eat?" he asked, caught in the theater of stupid assertion that was starting to become our marriage.

"Why do I *personally* need to eat?"

"Yeah."

"Because, if I don't eat," I said angrily, "I'm going to throw up from drinking too much."

When we got home, I hurled my purse across the kitchen floor. "I think maybe I should go see Earl," I said. Earl was Earl Gray, a matrimonial lawyer whom everyone in town called Mr. Tea. I believed myself to be unafraid of rupture. My engagement to Daniel had been years long and full of breakups.

"Fine," said Daniel, and we stood there, in the fluorescent light, greenish and out of our minds. I got sharp-tongued and judgmental, an unfortunate but necessary combination. In the beginning was the Word, and it was a reproachful one. "I can't stand this," I said finally, "not knowing what you do, with whom, what it means. I can't live like this. It's like living with a wolf in the cellar as a pet—except he's not a pet, in fact he's not even a wolf, he's a nuclear power plant!" I was drunk. "One of those shoddily constructed ones!" I marched over and threw open the basement door in some kind of attempt at illustration if not proof. "How many other women have there been? I want to know the truth! The truth!"

He was still and silent and sorry for me. Then he said, "I can't tell you the truth."

"What do you mean you can't tell me the truth? Why can't you tell me?"

"Because you'd be shocked," said Daniel. A look of bemused surliness came over him. "Not *surprised*—just shocked."

I lunged. I swung at him with both fists, and he threw me off with such fury and determination that I stumbled backward, into the open stairwell to the basement, my feet hitting air, my whole body falling, pitching backward toward the wolf and the nuclear power plant, the world reeling, both slow and fast, a tiny rectangle of light with Daniel in it, and then just the dark space of the basement, the pummeling thud of the steps and my hip and head and shoes, scraping and sliding, and finally me at the cement bottom, on my side, in shock, saying "Whoops, wope, whoops."

Perhaps there was some bit of expectedness, foreseeability, in it; even bad behavior must fall within some unconscious expectation in order for it not to seem monstrous.

Afterward, Daniel apologized and cried and visited me for hours every day in the hospital. Performing the sweet rituals that would keep us together; he knew I could not otherwise take him back. Once the penance is performed, at least at first, one has no choice. "Think of all those good, praying people who keep God around for the rest of us," said Daniel, on his knees by my bed. "God has no choice; he must honor the rites; if it were just the rest of us riffraff down here, he'd be long gone. But he comes through because of the good ones. He honors the covenant, the vows. Think of yourself as God. Think of me as the moral mix that is all of humanity."

"Oh, please."

"Well, then, think of me as—what? I don't know."

"You know those cream puffs called Divorce?" I say now to Marguerite.

"I've seen them."

"They're so totally great. Can we get those around here?"
Once, last year in Chicago, I was at a dinner party where a
newlywed woman kept interrupting her husband to say in a
theatrical whine, "Honey, can we get our *divorce* now? *Now*
can we get our divorce?" I was the only one there who
thought she was funny. I was the only one there who laughed
every time. At the end of the night, she leaned forward by
the door and kissed me on the lips.

"Sure! I know of a pretty good *pâtisserie* not far from
here." Marguerite's walk is strong and loping, impossible to
match. We stop at her *pâtisserie*, wildly order two Divorces,
then sit outside at the neighboring *tabac* drinking *panachés*
(half *bière*, half *limonade*) to go with them. "Isn't Paris amazing?" says Marguerite. "Where else would you have something like a *tabac*, half bar, half office supply store? The thing
about France is that from romance to food to whatever, they
really know what goes together. Look at all the red and
purple—look at the gardens and lobbies and scarves. Not every culture knows that red and purple go so well together."
She pauses. "Of course, it's also a totally sexist country."

"C'est dommage," I say, my mouth full of Divorce. I mention the men looking around, the libidinous, headlit bath the
Frenchwomen are swimming in.

"The worst thing, though," says Marguerite, "is when a
man walks by you in the street, sizes you up, and says, '*Pas
mal.' Pas mal!* You feel outraged in a hundred different direc-
tions." She pauses. "For one, you expect a little grade infla-
tion on the streets."

I laugh in a giddy way. I've eaten too much sugar. Marguerite orders water—"Château Chirac"—(a Parisian joke everyone knows, apparently, because it is scarcely acknowledged
as a joke). The waiter barely cracks a smile and then goes off

to the kitchen. Château Chirac is no longer funny; it is water; it is what water is called; it is what water is. And it makes me wonder how many things have begun this way, as jokes. Love, adolescence, marriage, life, death; perhaps God is looking down saying, "Geeze, y'all, lighten up. This is *funny*. You're missing the into*nation*!"

"I can't give my heart away to anyone but you," Daniel said to me in the hospital. "Not that I haven't tried, of course. It's just that when I do, the other organs start a letter-writing campaign."

"Don't be clever," I said. "Don't be like that now."

"What is your favorite painting in all of Paris?" I ask Marguerite. The liter of water has come and we gulp it down. She looks refreshed.

"Let me think," she says. She names Géricault, van Gogh, Picasso.

"All the *O*s," I say.

"All the *O*s! Actually, at the d'Orsay, there's a pastel of Madame Monet, with the ribbons of her hat all untied. That's probably my favorite. She's sitting on a bright blue sofa—the most beautiful blue you've ever seen—and she is looking straight out of the drawing, as if to say, 'I married a painter, and I still got this sofa.' I like that one. Very French."

"Do you think the Venus de Milo looks like Nicolas Cage?"

"A little," she says, smiling. "But you've got to remember: even with all her handicaps and shyness, she's lived in Paris; she's been gazed upon by Parisians for years, so she believes—a belief as good as gold—that she's absolutely beautiful."

"*Absolutely beautiful?*"

"Cute. OK. She thinks she's *cute*. She thinks she's so *goddamn* cute."

"Don't you hate that? Even in a statue, I just hate that."

We wander off to other galleries, where Marguerite shows me what she likes: big, broad, energetic paintings. "Sexy ones," she says.

At a show of collages—tiny, fussy, intricate little cuttings and pastings, ink squiggles, swatches of color—I go from one to the other, slow and fascinated, but Marguerite is bored. She comes up behind me. "See, I don't really like these," she says. "They're not *sexual*."

I turn and look at her. "See, to *me*, these are totally sexual," and then we both burst out laughing, our laughs booming in the gallery where others are whispering as if it were church.

"They're sexual maybe—like a foot fetish is sexual," says Marguerite.

"Exactly," I say. *"Exactement."*

Afterward we hike up to Père-Lachaise to look at Jim Morrison's grave, where there is a constant beer party, and where so many bottle caps have been mashed and pounded into the dirt they have made what looks like a carpet of coins. Over the sound of one badly tuned guitar, strummed by a barefoot German, Marguerite tells me that what she'd really like to do is make films. She knows the film she'd like to make—stories of Algerians in 1962: how they were herded outside Paris in camps; how many of them were killed, disappeared. How even now, on the outskirts of Paris, Africans in bright ski pants work the toxic jobs, the factories and power plants, how Paris is built and running on the backs of these people, on the back of abominable history. The Nazis, well: Everyone knows about the Nazis.

There is no place to put such facts, not properly. There is only one's own mournful horror, one's worthless moral vanity—which can do nothing. The bad news of the world, like most bad news, has no place to go. You tack it to the bulletin board part of your heart. You say *look*, you say *see*. That is all.

". . . So if this production company comes through, that is what I'd like to do, work with some of these documentary people," says Marguerite, "and make that film."

"Marguerite," I say. "That's great." *That's great.* "You must."

From Horsehearts to Paris, I think, staring at the ceiling. Has anyone even put those two places in the same thought before?

"I've been thinking about our genes," says Daniel, when I ask him how the day's conference events went. We are in bed, and it's hard to sleep. There are car alarms, motorcycle alarms, disco noises. A woman in the street below is singing, "Eef I ken mek eat there, all mek eat onywhere, eats op too you, New York, New York."

"Yes," I say.

"I mean, maybe it's all for the best. Besides the Tay-Sachs. Look at the genes. On your side there's diabetes and bad hearts."

"And bad blood."

"That's right. Bad blood. And on my side there's, well—"

"There's arrogance and not listening," I say.

"Arrogance and not listening." He laughs in a sighing way. "Did you have a good day with Marguerite? What are you thinking about?" he asks. "Was it fun? Don't worry. I can have this whole conversation by myself. You can just watch."

"I really like Marguerite," I say.

"I know you do."

I sigh, clutch the covers up under my chin.

"That's it? That's all that's on your mind?"

"Also *Manon Lescaut*," I say. Last week we saw a production of it at the Bastille.

"*Manon Lescaut?*"

"I'd like to die like that," I say. "All my jewelry on, and singing about madness."

"You would?"

"With all my jewelry on? Sure." Probably, in real life, I would die in a bathrobe, the telephone cradled in my neck.

"Do I know you?" asks Daniel. "You don't even wear jewelry."

"Yes, I do."

"A watch. You wear a watch. Lots of lipstick and a watch."

"It's a nice watch."

"It's gorgeous," Daniel says now sleepily. The air in our room is damp from the rains; it has turned my hair strumpety and full, but has made Daniel's skin moist and pale, color in his cheeks coming only in the day, outside, in the hurried pace to and from drier destinations. He seems delicate and young beside me.

I keep talking. "You know, *that's* one thing Manon wasn't wearing: a watch. You don't see a lot of watch wearing in the soprano world. Have you ever noticed that? Tosca? No watch. Madame Butterfly? Again, no watch."

He is no longer paying attention, but it doesn't stop me. We have traded places. "If in *La Bohème* you gave everyone wristwatches, you'd have a happy ending."

"You would?"

"Sure," I say. "You wouldn't have that guy singing about his coat. He'd look at his watch and go 'Yikes!'"

"Now that's what I'd like to hear. A nice aria with the word 'yikes' in it."

Daniel has never really liked opera. "What I like is philosophy," he said to me once. "Philosophy's great. Except I don't like the whole Existence thing. *Do we exist?* That really pisses me off. But I like Good and Evil. I like What is Art. But just a little of What is Art. If you get too much it circles back around again to *Do we exist?*, which pisses me off."

"I'm not really looking forward to going home," I say now.

"Really?"

"I feel disconnected these days, in the house, in town. The neighbors say, 'Hello, how are you?,' and sometimes I say, 'Oh, I'm feeling a little empty today. How about you?' "

"You should get a puppy," he says sleepily.

"A puppy?"

"Yeah. It's not like the cat. A puppy you can take for walks around the neighborhood, and people will stop and smile and say, 'Ooooh, look—What's *wrong* with your puppy?' "

"What *is* wrong with my puppy?"

"Worms, I think. I don't know. You should have taken him to the vet's weeks ago."

"You're so mean."

"I'm sorry I'm not what you bargained for," Daniel murmurs.

I stop and think about this. "Well, I'm not what you bargained for, either, so we're even."

"No," he says faintly, "you are. You're what I bargained for."

But then he has fallen over the cliff of sleep and is snoring, his adenoids a kind of engine in his face, a motorized unit, a security system like a white flag going up.

THE FIRST few days of July Isabelle began to show up at odd times and just stand at my cash register, watching. She would do this for five minutes, then leave, go back to her office.

It was making me nervous. The park was crowded. The lines were long. I had stopped doing any money, except, well, once in a while, when Sils and I would decide to go out to dinner someplace fancy—the Lafayette Café, the General Montcalm Inn—where we would order surf 'n' turf and stingers and baked potatoes with sour cream.

Then, the second weekend of the month, something happened in the park, and Isabelle seemed briefly to have disappeared with her new concerns: the Lost Mine crashed.

The Lost Mine was a roller-coaster-style ride through a

dark tunnel up in the Frontier Village part of the park: lighted mannequins dressed as old miners made snarling robotic noises as the little five-car train you were in zipped by them. I had taken the ride twice that summer: once early on, with Sils, and then another time, only just the week before, by myself, on a break, what the heck. You weren't really supposed to do that, as an employee, but mostly no one was watching, and the guys running the rides didn't care. I don't really know what the thematic point of the ride was except to plunge you into darkness alongside a narrative involving people who had gotten lost in that same darkness, stuck there in time: If you entered the Lost Mine (all that was Mine is Lost!), you, too, could become a trapped ghost, the worst kind of ghost, though of course the most common. Somehow I liked it. It made me feel that I was availing myself of whatever excitement there was in the world.

At dusk on the seventh of July one of the cars derailed inside the mine. From the main gate I first heard the dull banging sound, and five minutes later one of the other cashiers came rushing back from her break to tell me. "The Lost Mine!" she gasped. I took my break right then, emptied the drawer into the box, locked the register, and lugged my money box, went up there, along the Jack and Jill path, arriving in time to see a flashing ambulance in front of the entrance to the ride, long streaks of blood being hosed out of the wrecked train by the grounds crew, and the owner—the legendary Frank Morenton himself—standing there in his white hair and white shoes, his presence startling in the deepening dusk. He was quietly writing someone a check.

The small crowd that had gathered was being asked by some of the cowboys (the ones who staged the bank robbery every noon, the romance of theft and sun, how I knew it!) to disperse, please. Everything was fine, they said firmly, bowlegged in their chaps, their hats pushed to the very back of their heads. Everything was under control. One of the cowboys was Markie Russo, the one who'd had a crush on Sils last year.

Since I had five minutes left to my break, I went and lay on the grassy hill near the Shoot-Out Corral, where there were pony rides for the children. Cashiers were not supposed to sprawl about on the grounds like that, wander into sections where they were out of context, out of character, but once in a while you could get away with it. You could saunter aimlessly into the wrong story—a situation that, in real life, I thought, actually happened all the time. There was Randi, as Little Bo Peep, constantly going over to Jungle Safari to talk to a boy there she liked. There was Sils, who one day had to flee the palace grounds to mooch a cigarette from Alice in Wonderland. And there was me: I got to take this money box wherever I went; I got to hang out with Sils, and change in the ladies' locker room; I briefly got to feel that all that mattered was here and now in Horsehearts, though I was a worrier, a candy eater, a getter of canker sores.

I turned my head to read the fake western gravestones that had been placed on this side of the hill at angles calculated for a look of decrepitude. I could make out only one of the inscriptions: *Leadfoot Fred. Danced too slow and now he's dead.* Over the lake, days late, fireworks began—no doubt, as a distraction. (Pay no attention to that catastrophe in Frontier Village!) I watched as they exploded in the navy blue sky: a star, a heart, electric sea creatures, glittery bell skirts, garnet tarantulas—the delayed boom of each like something witty, and the whistling, zigzag ones so much like the surface of war that they scared me. Perhaps someone had really died. I grabbed up the money box, and headed back to my register.

The next day there was no word of the bloody Lost Mine

crash in the local Horsehearts paper, and not the next day, either, though the rumor among the ride operators was that a boy had lost his legs. "Morenton wrote the parents a check for a million dollars," Randi whispered to me at lunch, and I began to understand—again, anew—the cleansing power of money. By the end of a week the Lost Mine was functioning again, and the accident existed only as a persistent rumor, and then by the end of the month a less persistent one, and then a story, as if from long ago.

On my day off, in the afternoon, I went to Sils's house, the place athrob with her brothers' band in the basement, the drums and electric guitars vibrating the windows and screens. Just back from Canada, her brother Kevin, tall with bristly, ochre hair, came up from the basement, to look at the kitchen clock and take a pill. ("He times his drugs," Sils had said. "Maybe that's good.") He saw me at the screen door and sauntered over. He was wearing blue-tinted wire rims and a paisley vest with no shirt underneath. He was potbellied, and his skin was white, amphibious, strange with swirls of hair.

"Is Sils here?" I asked through the screen.

"Little Sils?" he repeated, mockingly, lightly, as if both she and I were small, amusing mammals. "Sure," he said, and without opening the door himself, he simply turned and bellowed, "Sils! Your friend's at the door for you!" and went back down into the cellar, from which came the steady, whining rock of a guitar solo, then the deep beat of the electric bass, vibrating the windows, frame and sash, straining the glass. It was good the Chaussées lived next door to a cemetery.

Sils came down the wide, gray-painted stairs of their house. "Hi!" she said, and out of the blue gave me a hug. "Are you hungry? I'm starved," she said.

"Sure," I said, determined, always, to be helpful. We went into the kitchen and hunted around. Her mother hadn't gone grocery shopping in weeks and there was nothing to make a salad or a sandwich with, and so we did as we often did: contented ourselves with raw potatoes, oleo, and salt— the potatoes cut in quarters and peeled, a meal of sororal resourcefulness. We sprinkled them with salt and spread difficult gobs of margarine along the edges. It was, in fact, a snack I loved: the cold bright fat of the Parkay, the apple-cool of the potato; our teeth gliding silently in, then noisily executing the bite through the potato. The damp crunch held a kind of comfort for me, the salt rubbing grainily against my gums. We ate raw potatoes a lot at her house—both in her room upstairs and at the beat-up aluminum dinette set in the kitchen.

This time we took them upstairs. We sat around a whole plate of them, on her rug, and felt mildly, mockingly bored by our own self-sufficiency. The afternoon was sunny and the light was angled already, spilling through the lattice outside her window, forming diamonds on the wall.

"Diamonds," I said. "Not my best suit."

"Hearts. I like hearts." She looked a little tired.

"How are you feeling?" I asked.

Sils lit up a cigarette. "Not so bad. I had cramps, but they're over."

"That's good. Can I bum a smoke?"

Sils handed over a cigarette. A look of anguish passed over her face. "You'll never guess what I found."

"What?" I filled my lungs with smoke, but felt it best, most comfortingly around my tongue and teeth.

Sils gulped a little and winced. "A piece of purple skin in my underwear," she said.

The confused and stricken girl's face that had spilled

forth this phrase, her eyes grappling with mine in a panicked way, made me moan and turn aside.

"Oh, god," I said. And then, not knowing what else to say, I said, "When?"

"This morning," she said. She blew smoke out through her nostrils, then stubbed her cigarette out in the ashtray, took up a chunk of raw potato, and bit into it.

"Well, at least it's all over," I said. Joni Mitchell was keening "Little Green" on Sils's record player. Sils listened to that song all the time now, like some woeful soundtrack. The soprano slides and *oo*s of the the song always made us both sing along, when I was there. "Little green, be a gypsy dancer." Twenty years later at a cocktail party, I would watch an entire roomful of women, one by one and in bunches, begin to sing this song when it came on over the sound system. They quit conversations, touched people's arms, turned toward the corner stereo speakers and sang in a show of memory and surprise. All the women knew the words, every last one of them, and it shocked the men.

"Now, where were we?" everyone said when the song was over.

"You don't really like Mike, do you?" Sils asked now.

I felt caught. "I don't know," I said.

"Come on," she said. "You can tell me."

"It's just that . . . I don't know. He has no *texture*."

"He's got texture," said Sils. "You've just got to beat it out of him." She lit up another cigarette. "Which, I realize, you shouldn't have to do with texture."

"No," I said. "Not really."

Sils's eldest brother, Skip, the band's drummer, pulled up in the driveway, noisy and elegant in his way. Just back from Canada, too, he was in and out of the band; he also popped pills in the kitchen, looking at the clock, glugging white and red tablets down with beer. He had his girlfriend Diane with him. When the girlfriends were there, they and Sils's brothers took over the house, lying on top of one another on the living room sofas, kissing and rubbing and napping.

"Let's get out of here," said Sils, hearing Skip downstairs. She was working a late shift and didn't have to leave for an hour. Mike was picking her up. "Let's go for a walk." So we did. We left her house and walked around in the park, looking for arrowheads and puffballs, until it was time for her to go.

The next day at Storyland was slow—a warm drizzle keeping people away—and at about five o'clock Mike Suprenante drove up on his Harley. He took off his helmet and glided his motorcycle up to my register.

"Would you like a ticket, *monsieur*?" I tried to be funny, friendly, but I sounded full of hate, even to my own ears.

"I want to see you alone to talk about Sils."

I looked at him, trying to let nothing show. I felt secretly pleased. He had, with this request, acknowledged I was her guardian, her confidante, closer to her than he.

"When can we do that?" he asked sternly.

I felt powerful. "I don't know. Tonight, maybe."

Herb, the manager, came up and stood behind the ticket tearer's gate. "Get that thing outta here," he said angrily, in the direction of the motorcycle.

Mike started to back it up, slowly.

"You'd better move faster than that," said Herb. "We can't have vehicles in the main entrance of the park."

Mike looked at me. "Ten o'clock. Out front here," he called out. "*Ça va?*"

"Yeah," I said, my voice hickish and tough.

Mike glided backward, then turned, started up his bike,

and left. Herb came through the gate, then just stood next to me, frowning. I stood there, saying nothing, shifting my weight from one hip to the other.

"*What?*" I said finally, impudently.

"No more pals" is all he said. "No more." And then he smiled falsely, a grimacing stack of teeth, and walked pompously away.

"Do you want to go have a drink?" Mike asked me at closing time in front of the main gate to Storyland. It had stopped raining and the night sky had cleared. There was a bar down the road called Fort Ress, owned by a guy named Dickie Ress, and Mike liked to go there. Or there was the Sans Souci.

"All right," I said.

"Wanna go to the Ress?"

"OK."

"Wanna hop on?"

"No. I'll walk." It was a five-minute walk past the public beach to the Ress.

"Whatever," said Mike. He grinned. "I'll get us a good table out on the patio. The one with the least bird turd." He grinned again.

I narrowed my eyes. "Promises, promises," I said. No matter what the situation, a sarcastic tone was a Horsehearts girl's best response.

Mike winked and roared off ahead. "The *vroom-vroom* gene," Sils had said the day the exhaust pipe on Mike's Harley burned a scar into her leg. "All boys are born with it. *Vroom-vroom.*"

I trudged up the road. It was after ten o'clock at night, and the sky was still a bluish color and peepers sang from the trees in the park. A frog chorus. *The frogs sing for no reason and so do we* went a line from a poem I had learned in school, and I imagined these frogs now scattered through the woods, their tiny eyes lit like chips of emerald, while their pumping whistle-chant—part summons, part yearning lullaby—piped through the night. *Whoops, wope, who-wopes.* I felt accompanied, guarded, by the throb and thrum of it, as I hiked along the beach road up toward the lights of Marvy's Miniature Golf, where, when I got there, I could no longer hear the peeping—only bar noise and golfers in wide-lipped hats.

The frogs. Years later, I would read in the paper that frogs were disappearing from the earth, that even in the most pristine of places, scientists were looking and could not find them. It was a warning, said the article. A plague of no frogs. And I thought of those walks up the beach road I'd made any number of times in the sexual evening hum of summer, how called and lovely and desired you felt, how *possible*, even when you weren't at all. It was the frogs doing that. Later it seemed true, that I rarely heard frogs anymore. Once in a while a cricket would get trapped on the porch, but that was all. That was different. We would find it with a broom and sweep it off.

At the Ress, I sat outside with Mike on the patio. He'd already brought beers to the table in large waxed cups. Plus two shots of whiskey for himself.

"I know," he said. He threw back one of the whiskeys.

"Know *what*?" I asked.

"Sils told me. About the baby." At the word "baby" he threw back the second shot. It was very dramatic.

"What baby?"

"The one you went to Vermont with. Sils told me. She told me she'd been pregnant. She told me everything."

"There was no *baby*," I said finally.

The whiskey was doing its work. Mike leaned forward,

hunched over the empty shot glasses, maudlin and drunk, unrolling the waxy rim of his beer cup with his thick fingers. "I would have taken care of it. I would have brought up that kid." He began to blubber. I was only fifteen, and he was nineteen. But he seemed mawkish and ridiculous to me. Why had Sils told him? I'd thought the whole point had been not to tell him.

"Get off it," I said. "Get on with things." *Get a life*, I might have said, but it wasn't an expression yet. Instead I repeated the words of my sixth-grade teacher the day she'd spied my lipstick. "You're too young," I said, getting it down, slowly, like a chant.

"Ha!" he cried out. But his teariness subsided a bit, and he began to smile a little awkwardly and try to flirt with me. He rubbed my head with one of his big hands like a paw. "You've got a lot on the ball," he said. "Plus, you know what? My friend Arnie thinks you're cute." He grinned again, with this hot, funny news. "What do you think?"

I couldn't even remember who Arnie was. "I've gotta get going," I said, finishing my beer. I didn't want to remember who Arnie was. I didn't want to meet Arnie, or talk to him, or have him try to touch me. I didn't want anyone to touch me. There was nothing to touch.

"You're a good friend," he said. "You're Sils's best friend. So, in a way, I've always considered you mine as well."

I felt revulsed.

"Can I give you a ride home?" His speech was slurred and his grin now snaked across his face in a demented way that someone somewhere had probably told him was fetching.

It was ten miles back to Horsehearts.

"I'm calling a cab," I said.

"Oh, the *cab* guy?" Mike piped up gleefully, to let me

know he knew. "With your little *moola?*" He held his hand in the air and rubbed his thumb against his fingers. God, had Sils told him *everything?*

"Sure, sure."

I went inside the Ress and used the phone.

"Oh, you again," said Humphrey. "How the heck are you?"

"I'm up at the lake, corner of Beach and Quaker is how I am."

"Need a ride?"

"Yup."

"I'll be there."

"Thanks," I said.

I checked my wallet. I was running low. Perhaps I'd have to do more money at work tomorrow. Just once more, and then that would be it. Then I'd stop forever.

I went back and sat at the table across from Mike, waiting for my ride. The Ress had strung chili-pepper lights above and across the patio section of this place, but there was no one sitting out here in the buggy night but us, and the forced exuberance of the lights seemed mocking and depressing. Steppenwolf blared from the jukebox inside.

"Are you going to stay here or go back in, or what?"

"Aw. Are you concerned?" he asked.

I didn't say anything.

"Arnie'll probably show up later," he said teasingly.

"Where's Sils tonight?" I asked.

"Ha! It only took you an hour to ask. I must be having some success with you. Do you realize I never used to be able to say two words to you without you twisting around going 'Where's Sils?' "

Now I just looked past Mike out toward Beach Road. I stared out into the night, in silence, until I could see Humphrey driving slowly past in his cab, looking for me.

"Gotta go," I said. I waved. I patted him on the hand, squeezed his shoulder. Nobody kissed cheeks then; it would have been a joke.

"Yeah, *go*," said Mike, some new blame in his voice. "Yeah, go on in your expensive little Killer Cab."

"Oh, Christ," I said, and turned on my heels and left, trotted out toward the intersection, waving a hand to signal Humphrey, who was now turning around and driving back toward the Ress parking lot.

"Where's your friend?" he asked when I got in.

"It's just me tonight," I said. At last I had a man driving *me*, waiting down the street just for *me*, though of course I had to pay him.

The next morning it was eighty degrees by seven o'clock. We were in a heat wave; all the fans my parents owned were on and swirling the thick air around our house. At seven-thirty the phone rang, and I stumbled out into the hallway to get it.

"What did you tell Mike last night?" It was Sils. Her voice was chilly but edged with hysteria.

"I don't know. I don't think I told him anything. What did he tell you? What did *you* tell *him*?"

"Arnie just called. He said last night you and Mike met for drinks and afterward he was drinking and yelling loudly. He took off half-cocked and got into an accident on his motorcycle." Here Sils began to cry in a light, shell-shocked way. "He's in intensive care with tubes and everything. He might die."

Mike: what a stupid jerk. "Oh, my god," I said instead. The car and motorcycle accidents of the local Horsehearts boys were the staple of the community news and drama. Yet I had never known anyone who had been killed, or anyone who had died, not really, not well. My grandfather had died when I was three, but I couldn't remember it.

"Is he conscious?" was all I could think of to say.

"No." Now something caught in Sils, something realized, and she began to cry in an insistent, bleating way. "I've got to go see him."

It was a three-mile walk to the county hospital. "I'll call Humphrey," I said. "I'll have him meet us by the park pond at what—nine o'clock? That way we won't have to walk in this heat. You won't be all sweaty and gross when you see Mike." I don't know why I said the last part; I just threw it in.

"Berie, he's *unconscious*," she said sternly.

"I *know that*," I said. Nothing anyone said that morning made any sense to me.

Thus began a two-week period when, every other day, either before or after Storyland, and always on our days off, in the sweltering heat, we took Humphrey's cab to the county hospital, stayed for an hour, then phoned Humphrey again and had him come pick us up. This let my mother off the hook a bit ("I'm getting a ride to work with Sils and her brother," I'd call from the front door), but it took money. So I managed to acquire a little extra at my register.

After two days Mike had returned to consciousness, "or his version of it," I said to Sils, and in her relief she actually laughed; by the second week he was giving Sils come-hither looks, saying things like "Gedover 'ere, you," wanting her to snuggle next to him amid the tubes.

I got in a wheelchair and for fun trundled up and down the corridors. Mike and Sils shared an understanding, newly worked out in Mike's hospital bed, amid the sheets and TV and bad fluorescent lighting, that the accident had been caused by a combination of her abortion and a truck.

I didn't say a word. I zoomed up and down the hallways in the wheelchair, nodding good morning to everyone. I smiled in a cheerful but authoritative manner. One time I accidentally backed into an elevator and went all the way down to the lobby. Once I was there, I decided to see how far I could go. I pushed through the revolving door. I hit the street.

No one stopped me. I wheeled myself halfway downtown—past the hospital gardens, past the guest houses and the Grand Union and the junior high. I even tried a wheelie off the curb, which spilled me out into the street and scraped my knee, but still no one was looking. Finally, I turned around and pushed the thing back. I stopped at the Grand Union and got a Coke.

"Your father's worried about you," my mother said to me one night, in her nightgown, standing over me in a looming way.

"Dad?" I was clipping my toenails, sending hard yellowed crescents flying through the room with each clip.

"Will you stop that while I'm speaking to you? Have you no respect for anything?" She stepped in from the doorway and swatted my thigh.

"What?" I looked up. Her formerly bleached blond hair was now a tigerish mix of black and white; she was getting a mustache. Her hazel eyes flashed with hate.

"When I bring you to or from work, you're sullen in the car, half the time we don't see you at dinner, you haven't spoken to your father or brother or LaRoue for weeks, or been to church in months, and how about your grandmother? Have you taken the time to go visit her? She doesn't have *that* much longer to live, you know!"

My Grandmother Carr lived in a large Victorian house in the middle of Horsehearts. It was a house full of what my grandmother called "davenports" and "chesterfields." "Don't put your feet on the chesterfield, dear."

"You mean the *couch*," my brother, Claude, always said, to be rude.

There were three cellos in the house; one had belonged to my grandfather. The other two belonged to my grandmother, who often gave lessons in town, and whenever we visited she got out one of the cellos and played a piece for us, while we sat on one of the davenports, squirming and pinching each other when she couldn't see. Later, when I was older, I realized how beautifully she'd played. But when I was little, most of the interest such an event held for me was in watching such a formal woman—"a true Victorian lady," as my father worshipfully described her—place this large woman-shaped object between her legs and hold it there with her knees, her finger vibrating along the neck in an insectlike movement up and down, the bow in a slow saw across the strings, angling this way or that, gently, to find the note. My grandmother always gazed down upon her cello, like the Holy Mother upon the Holy Child, or perhaps like one woman beholding another at her knees.

"Are you done?" Claude was often the first to ask, and my grandmother would smile with a kind of wan forgiveness and say, "Yes. I'm done."

"I'll go see her soon," I said now to my mother. I'd made such a promise before, but what the heck: I made it again.

"And," my mother continued, "Mrs. Lollick at church would like you to come help in the nursery again." The year before, every third Sunday, while my parents attended the service, I had helped baby-sit in the Baptist church nursery—a large pink room with cribs at one end; at the other hung an enormous gold-framed painting of Jesus, whose upward gaze and caramel-colored locks gave him the look of a dewy Kenny Loggins. This alone made helping in the nursery better than sitting out in the sanctuary listening to the service, surrounded by old women in wool felt hats with fishnetty little veils, long furry animals draped heads and paws and all around the collars of their coats. During the sermons, I had always stared at the bright stained glass—Jesus as Shepherd—and, in my mind, recolored it, in head shop blacks and mauves. My parents had become Baptists after they had married, leaving the Catholic and Episcopalian churches for something they'd felt was more suited to them. Now they never missed a week. They sang in the choir. They ushered. They prayed.

"All right," I said. "I'll phone her."

"And that's not even my main point here," said my mother. "The main point is that you seem drifty and unfocused."

"*What?*" I grinned up at her and crossed my eyes. It was the sort of response I might have made to Sils, whom it would have cracked up, but to my mother it was only impudence.

She leaned over and slapped me hard across the face. "You heard me," she said, and slammed the door.

Once, I went too far with the wheelchair; I went all the way downstreet, stopping and staring in the store windows. It was early morning, and no one was there. By the time I got back to the hospital, Sils had already left.

"Sils left," said Mike. "She didn't know where you'd gone."

"I was outside, fooling around with the wheelchair."

"She thought maybe you got sick of waiting."

"Oh, well."

"Yeah. Oh, well. She didn't know. She had to go to work."

"So do I," I said. Now I'd have to call my mother. Or a cab. "So, I should go myself." Mike looked recovered to me. Confident and condescending in that boy way, that way that illness and injury usually eradicated. But now it was back. He was off the glucose drip. He was watching a lot of TV. "I'm glad you're better," I said.

"Are you?" He grinned, in, that strange lopsided style he had.

"Sure. What do you mean?"

"I mean, here's me, all laid up in the hospital, and there's you—probably with your lezzy fantasies—"

"What are you talking about, you pig?"

"I'm talking about you with Sils, how you act like . . . I don't know. I'm just wondering. Thinking out loud."

I picked up my big rope purse, which I'd left by the nightstand, and walked out.

"Oh, come on," I could hear him saying behind me. "I didn't mean anything."

Isabelle, Herb, my mother, now Mike Suprenante getting on my nerves. My life like an old turnip: several places at once going bad. The next night it was Isabelle again. She called me up to her office, a large, polka-dotted room above the main entrance. I sat down in the card-table chair in front of her desk.

"What's going on with your register?"

"What do you mean?" I was tense and held my back straight as a board.

"Sometimes you're short, sometimes you're over. Are you locking the register and taking the key on your lunch hour?"

"Yes."

"Are you emptying the drawer and taking the money box with you on breaks?"

"Mostly," I said.

She looked at me sternly. She wore spike heels and nylons, even in the direst heat, and I could hear one of her legs swing scratchily back and forth. "Don't do that anymore," she said about the money box. "We're not going to do that anymore."

"OK."

"We're going to put you over at the Lakeside entrance tomorrow."

The Lakeside entrance was unknown to most of the tourists, and so it was always slow there. The times I'd worked there before I'd spent the whole time writing Sils a long note on a spare roll of orange ticket tape. The note had been full of jokes about Stan the security guard and Mary at the gift shop having an affair.

But there was no one to tear tickets there—you tore them yourself—so it was the easiest place of all the registers to sell stubs.

I sat out there by myself that day, writing Sils a note. *Hey, bébé,* it began, in the same imbecilic way as all the others. *What you say we meet for a smokin' good time tonight?*

"Is this an entrance to the amusement park?" asked a middle-aged couple with a young boy.

They read the prices on the board outside. "He's only two," said the woman, pointing at the boy. "And he's only what, eleven?" She pointed to her husband.

"You're only two?" I studied the boy, who was at least eight.

He shrugged. "I guess."

"All right," I said.

"And how about *me?*" asked the man. He was wearing white shoes, a white golf shirt, and sky-blue pants. His neck and arms were sunburned and corded with veins. "I'm only two, too."

"Mentally he's only two," said his wife.

Once you had seen enough people go through your register you realized everyone was the same: they looked the same, said the same things; they were all the same.

All the same, I scribbled large on my current ticket-tape note to Sils, right in front of them; *full of the stupidities that obviously keep their marriage going.* I wrote in a careful, loopy script, waiting as they tried to figure out how old they were.

I looked out through my window at the boy. "If you're not as tall as that sign and at least nine years old," I said, "you won't be able to go on the rides alone. It has to do with the park's insurance policy." No doubt he'd be back for a "grow-up," a system Herb had devised to let kids come back to the cashier and pay the difference in admission so they could ride the rides alone. "We've got a grow-up here," he liked to say, ushering some boy to the register. "We've got a boy here who suddenly, magically grew up."

There was money in grow-ups. When no one was looking, you just wrote "grow-up" on a stub, stuck it in the register, and took out the price of a child's ticket.

"I know," said this boy now, looking unhappy and trapped.

"Two adults and an under-six," the couple said to me.

"That's twenty dollars forty cents," I said, not pressing any numbers, just pressing No Sale and letting the drawer pop out with a *brrinnng.*

"How much?" the man asked. He kept looking past the Plexiglas window, trying to get a view of the register total. But the numbers only said "0.00."

"Twenty dollars forty cents," I repeated. He gave me the exact change, which I temporarily placed in the register, shutting the drawer. Later, I would take it out.

"There you go," I said, handing them three ticket stubs. "Keep your tickets for the rides."

They frowned and waved and pushed their way through the turnstile, then turned the corner into the park and disappeared.

I waited a while before I rang the drawer open to take out the money. I waited to see if I heard anyone, someone just inside the entrance, someone crouching in a bush, someone lurking behind the cashier's booth, perhaps, where I couldn't see: someone with a walkie-talkie, or maybe just Stan the security guard on a cigarette break. But there seemed to be nobody, nothing, just the usual distant happy cries of kids, and so I rang the drawer open and then when I looked up over the register I saw Isabelle out of nowhere in her angry clicking spike heels, rounding the corner by the Baa-Baa Black Sheep Petting Pen and walking briskly toward the entrance. She was followed by Herb, who looked red-faced and vexed, and a policeman looking bored but stern—in a professional way. Isabelle pushed through the exit turnstile and knocked on my glass with her knuckles.

"OK," she said, "close up this register. We're shutting down this entrance." Then she came to the side of my booth, unlocked the door, and pulled it open. With a sweep of her arm, she ushered me out. I pushed the register drawer shut and did as I was told. My chest was pounding. I was in trouble. *That family,* I thought. *They were spies, plants, part of some in-house detective scheme.* The nausea of all the rides—the spinning teacups, the whirling Black Widow—entered me, and I turned momentarily away in a sweat. My heart beat in a loud panic, and I struggled to breathe normally.

"We've been examining the numbers on the stubs from this register." Isabelle was a fierce statue of righteousness, her arm was still hanging in the air, pointing out toward the park. In my quick, flooding fright, I felt puny and liquid, the only remedy for which was disbelief. I filled my head with so much disbelief I became dizzy and mad with it. Stan the security guard stepped impassively into the entranceway— from where? from nowhere—and lit up a cigarette in a sly and fraught way. Stan: it had been him!

For a crazed moment, with Isabelle locking up the register and Herb putting up the This Entrance Closed sign, I tried to make a break for it. I stuffed the note to Sils in my pinafore pocket, and brushing quickly past Herb and Stan in the now crowded little entrance, I dashed out the turnstile and sprinted toward the far fence near the gift shop, its Storyland thermoses and T-shirts shining in the window. I headed for those, my afternoon shadow beneath me like a puddle, like some strange pair of dark snowshoes fitted backward. I would run through the store, then out Memory Lane into the parking lot. I'd hide behind cars, then hitch a ride. "Hey!" shouted the county cop and Herb. My straw hat flew off me. I ran faster, then something locked in my knee, my ankle twisted, and I fell, the ground flying up in my face. I lay there for a second. What was I thinking of? That I could escape? Become a fugitive? Isabelle and the men were running toward me. I sat up, and faced them, wiping grass and dirt from my elbows and legs. "I'm sorry," I said. I lifted my hands in surrender, and then in a shrug. Herb and Isabelle yanked me up by the arms and I stood and went with them. People had stopped and were looking, the whole surreal world in a hot, bright leer like an Italian movie. I'd seen an Italian movie once with Sils.

"Hold her tight," said Stan to Herb, not unmusically, turning to go back to his post and putting his hat back on. He had, apparently, taken it off in the heat and hubbub. "Don't ever let her go."

On Isabelle's desk was a picture of her little girl, Gloria Deb. Isabelle had been divorced for years and she had had to work hard. Rumor had it that Frank Morenton gave her a shiny convertible every Christmas as a bonus, plus a trip to Florida.

Now Isabelle glared at me. So many things were on the line for her. "What did you *think* would happen?" she shouted.

"I don't know," I said.

The phone rang, and she picked it up. "Hello?" She listened for a moment. *"Elle a mangé la grenouille,"* she said, and then hung up. She has eaten the frog; she has nibbled the cash box. She looked at me, sighed, and scowled. She was momentarily wordless, as if due to a small, cerebral hemorrhage. I felt sorry for her. I decided, with a child's madness, to help her out. I forced a comical smile. "Well," I said, with manufactured lightness, "I suppose this is going to go on my permanent record."

She glared at me. "We're going to have to make an example out of you. I'll have to check with Mr. Morenton as to whether we'll prosecute. But certainly we will ask for reimbursement. How much have you taken altogether? A hundred? Two hundred? A *thousand?*" Her voice had acquired the fury of the betrayed, the divorced, the tired and working too hard.

Multiple choice. I always favored A. "A hundred," I said.

Herb glowered at me, but one could see he was having an exciting day.

Isabelle began to straighten the papers on her desk. "Deputy Kerry here, from the Sheriff's Department, will take you home in his police car. We'll phone your parents to let them know."

I started to cry. I broke and sobbed.

"Put the handcuffs on her," said Isabelle to the deputy.

The deputy gave us all a pitiful look. "I'm sure that's really not necessary, ma'am."

"Put them on her and march her right out the front door. We need this as an example to the others."

"All right, I guess," he said, shrugging. He turned toward me. "You are under arrest. Put your hands behind your back."

I was still crying, wiping my nose with the heels of my hands. I had no Kleenex, and no one would offer me one.

"Wait a minute," I mumbled, and made some final attempt to clear my face of snot, then stood, turned, and thrust my hands back toward the deputy, who had unfastened his handcuffs from his belt. They were cold and stiff, adjusted tight for my thin wrists. These are the hands that had taken money, the cuffs seemed to say, and we are going to seize them, take them out of commission, chop them off. "Oh, no," I moaned.

I was marched down the stairs and out through the front entrance, the deputy leading the way, grasping my elbow, and carrying my fallen straw hat, though it was Park Property. I was still wearing my cashier's uniform—Hello My Name Is Benoîte-Marie—and I was trying to hold back my tears by breathing them into my sinuses. It was four in the afternoon, and the heat of the day had gathered itself thickly, even as the sun—a hot blister of bone—had begun its descent.

"Oh, my god!" I heard Sheryl, at the left front register, gasp behind me.

"What happened?" asked Debbie.

"What's going on?" queried several Visitors to the Park, as we passed them standing in line. The loudspeakers played the Storyland theme song—now a bunch of *oom-pah-pahs* gone grim, like the end of *La Traviata.* Deputy Kerry marched me out in front of him, a light grip on my upper arm, and steered me straight across Storyland's bright, sunny parking lot, to the back, where his car was parked. In the side of my vision I could see Sils in her stainless-steel tiara and sateen dress, pressed to the wrought-iron fence next to where her Pumpkin Coach toured. She called my name, then kept calling it, but I refused to turn. I was ugly and embarrassed; there was snot dripping down into my mouth and I couldn't stop it. I didn't want anyone else to see me. I didn't want her to see. I twisted my neck and tried to wipe my nose on my shoulder, but I couldn't do it.

The entire way back to Horsehearts—me in the back, Deputy Kerry in the front—Deputy Kerry said scarcely a word. He drove steadily down the lake road, past the tee-pee–shaped gift shops selling their fake Indian trinkets, past the turquoise motels all clutched to the lakeshore as if they were contemplating hurling themselves in. What would it matter? Especially in the long winter when the world abandoned them anyway. My head was full of carcasses and ghosts.

Deputy Kerry received a call over his radio, and he picked up the mouthpiece and spoke into it. It reminded me of riding with Humphrey in his cab; only this was the sarcastic, perverted version. How much more complicated it was for me, just me, to get a guy to drive me home from the lake. See what great lengths I had to go to! See how much ingenuity and nerve! Ho-ho! Sils had it easy. All she had to do was smile. I had to steal and weep and take on the law.

"Where do you live?" asked Deputy Kerry as we neared the chipping, weather-beaten old Chamber of Commerce sign that read, tragicomically, Entering Horsehearts: Village of the Future. It seemed strange that Deputy Kerry was only asking me this now, where I lived. What if I'd said, "Oh, didn't they tell you? I live in Washington, D.C.!"

"Fish Glen Road," I said. "Three thirty-six."

"Oh, over there," he said cryptically, and took a left at the next light.

My parents were on the front porch when we pulled up. To my dim and watery eyes, they looked faraway, two pink and furious figurines, and I realized, slowing up in front of the house, swollen-faced and handcuffed, that I didn't know my parents well enough to be doing this to them, inflicting such an episode upon their lives. I realized that it was harder to endure the wrath and disappointment of people who've been kept from you, and from whom you've kept yourself, than it was to endure it from the people whom you knew best. All my stern upbringing was there waiting for me on the porch, its unhappy administrators waiting to administer something final and more—or perhaps, in their failure, to resign altogether, to take their leave of sternness, of administration, of me.

My mother stood up from the porch glider on which she'd been sitting, rocking herself back and forth with one foot, the other foot tucked up under her, her arms folded across her chest, her expression stricken and tight. My father turned from where he'd been gazing out into the mountains, rethinking his forestry degree, perhaps, or humming the most tragic Brahms he knew, or once again lamenting the snowmobiles that had wrecked the local wildlife, causing deer, now inured to the sound of motors, to dash out onto the highway and be killed. Perhaps he was making a list of all the ways your children could break your heart. He was not one to let you know what he was thinking, but he let you watch him think it, let you watch him stare into the air in which he constructed his worries and ideas, his eyes transfixed, his lips folded in. Now he turned to look at me, and the sheer height of him, even at that distance, filled me with remorse.

Deputy Kerry unlocked my handcuffs by the car but still clutched my elbow, pushing me along in front of him like a little cart. It was a long march during which I understood that, for all the unusualness in their lives, all my parents had ever wanted was to be average, normal, useful, ordinary. They could not bear the full force and chaos of their own eccentricity, could not bear the full life of it, the complete course, all the stuff and ramifications. To see something out of line in their own children must have reminded them of all that they were and could not hide from. It must have reminded them of the deep and sorrowful loneliness of themselves, which they had tried so desperately not to suffer.

Deputy Kerry handed me my hat.

"Go to your room," my mother said coldly, and I stepped obediently into the house, staring down at my own steps as I took them, like a cartoon of a shamed person.

"Whoa," said Claude, from inside the kitchen, seeing me. He was making a peanut butter and jelly sandwich. "What did you *do?*" he asked.

"Just—shush," I said miserably. I went into my room and flopped on my bed. I dashed the straw hat to the floor.

Claude came to the bedroom doorway. He bit into his

sandwich. "Don't worry," he said with his mouth full. "I'll spy for you; I'll let you know what's going on. I can check it all out from the front porch."

"Great," I said indifferently.

LaRoue came up from the cellar. *"Tsk, tsk,"* she said at my doorway. And then added, more consolingly, "Don't worry." She looked sorry for me, for the first time in her life. "Don't worry. I heard them talking. They've decided not to yell."

What they'd decided to do was to send me to church camp for the rest of the summer. They told me this after they'd thanked Deputy Kerry and shaken his hand (for a job well done?), and after they'd suddenly, briefly entertained a visit from Frank Morenton himself, who, Claude later told me, came flying up in his white convertible, leaping out to apologize to my parents for the public display at Storyland. He was also bearing my rope purse, which I had left at the Lakeside entrance. (How strange to imagine him with my purse!) "Let's keep this whole thing with your daughter just between us. Here, this belongs to her." He thrust the purse at my mother. "The park's a nice family place," he added. "I'm getting to be an old man. I've seen a lot. I came to this country with no money, and I worked too hard now to have my efforts be the site of scandal and commotion. I believe in America." I was being treated with the same anxious hands as the Lost Mine crash. I *was* the Lost Mine crash. I was the same thing. *All that is mine won't be lost.*

Saved by America.

"What country do you think he's from?" I asked Claude.

"Indonesia," Claude replied. "Or maybe France. How should I know?"

Later I heard that Frank Morenton had fired Isabelle for

her bad judgment, only to hire her back again the next day; I also heard she still got her car and her Christmas trip to Florida and that he bought Gloria Deb a bright red moped.

"Your daughter, of course, is fired," he said to my parents. "But as for the money, let's just call it even-steven." Horsehearts was the sort of place where even a person of prominence might say things like "even-steven." It was the sort of place where if you stayed too long, you might add or subtract syllables; you might ask for "ham*burgs*" or "cheese*burgs*" or "cream de *mint*." After twenty years, you could end up saying "bingo" for "yes."

"We greatly appreciate that," murmured my father.

"Would you care to come in for some ice tea?" asked my mother.

"No, thanks," said Frank Morenton. "I just wanted to hurry down here and tidy up, let you know that although I could, I'm not going to prosecute. Now we can just move on, put things behind us."

"Yes," said my mother.

"I hope you will do as I intend to do and not mention this to people."

After that my parents said nothing Claude could discern.

"Now I've got to get back," Morenton announced, and then he was gone, fast in his beautiful car, like a shiny, shiny god.

That's how Claude described it later. I'd stayed in my room, as told. I'd stared at my *Desiderata* poster. *Go placidly amid the noise and the haste. . . .*

Go placidly.

What a crock.

The camp was a Baptist one a hundred miles away in the mountains on Lake Panawauc, said my parents, standing in my bedroom not long after Frank Morenton had left. I would be sent there until the end of August. Then I'd come back and pack for fall and winter. They were sending me away to boarding school.

"A military academy?" I asked, and no one in the room, myself included, knew whether I was joking.

"The Mount Brookfield School," said my father. I was astonished that in my fifteen-minute ride from the lake to Horsehearts they had planned my future so specifically. "The financial arrangements we may have to work out with your grandmother. It would behoove you to pay her a visit and explain yourself."

"Yup," I said drily, "I guess it would." We were all standing in my pink and purple room, with the *Desiderata* poster and the beehive shade and the records and the makeup mirror. I started playing with the dangling string of the light switch, turning it on and off, watching the beehive shade fill up with pink, and then empty again to white, watching the pink when it threw itself across my parents' faces like a veil of embarrassment, then vanishing again like a passing fever, or the patrolling light from a squad car.

"What is *wrong* with you?" asked my father in a disgusted way, and I started to cry again because I didn't know.

He turned angrily and walked out of the room, and my mother hesitated, then followed, though she cast me back a look that in another story might have turned me to salt or caused me to disappear entirely. Instead, in this one, it just left me there with the pink light, a large black moth banging at the screen, the sound of the Naval Reserve officers unit during the supper hour marching down the street, performing their summer exercises with low hums and scuffs and heps, to save our country, our world, our freedom! I threw myself on the bed, weeping. I dreamed a disinformation dream of Cuba.

That August the Republican convention renominated Nixon; he was "winding down the war," like a kind of path.

Watergate was breaking.

Patty Duke got married.

A storm on the sun briefly remagnetized the earth.

I heard about these only in faint broadcasts from my counselor's radio during rest hour. I lay in the bunk above Monica Hyde, a fourteen-year-old from North Syracuse. When I couldn't hear the radio, I talked to her. Her biggest sin, she said, had been tearing the zipper off the Rolling Stones' *Sticky Fingers* album cover so she could see what was underneath.

"Oh, I did that," I said. "You were *supposed* to do that."

"No, you weren't," she said. And I would contemplate my tanned arms, or the previous night's vespers held in the cricket-chorused chapel (a cleared area of shore with log benches and Lake Panawauc itself as the pulpit). I passed the time being alternately bored and outraged by boredom, seeking new means of self-forgiveness and penance for my crimes. I fell slightly in love with the camp director's son, a boy my age named Hayden Filo who had been a thalidomide child and who had only three fingers and six toes. After vespers we would sometimes walk through the woods together and he would talk about God, never Jesus, never the Son! Just God, and what God wanted—in ways that sometimes made God seem as gorgeous and enveloping as the violet dusk in which we roamed, and other times like a spoiled and faraway child vexing all his relations.

Sometimes we stopped, by trees and rocks and forks in the path, and kissed. Tree crickets and katydids sang with the ceaseless squawk of a clothesline pulley, all that endless hanging of laundry in the night. *Please! We don't want to hear about it!* We lifted our hands and held each other's faces. We closed our eyes, then oddly, without warning, opened them again. We stayed up late and watched for the northern lights, which came a lot now because of the storm on the sun. They looked like car headlights flashed across the sky, and sometimes failed to impress us. Other times they seemed as miraculous as the angels and we could feel ourselves under their spell and full of kindness and light, our dark, accidental pasts far away.

I won a sword drill competition. I knew the Bible like my own closet (Leviticus 14:10! Green knit crochet vest!). Somehow it was all the same, all paraphernalia my brain had seized and catalogued in a kind of heartless, automatic way. My brain sought always to make the strange familiar, available, not scary. It built railings, ways to get around, maps and roads. It farmed and planted with a panicked, compulsive, mechanical energy. And so I won the Bible drills.

I came in second in a back-dive contest.

I sang "Were You There When They Crucified My Lord?" in a solo, in front of everyone, at Sunday service. At the end no one clapped, but you didn't at a church service. That was one of the things that was too bad about church.

I wrote long letters to Sils, making up grotesque but harmless accounts of the other girls in my tent—"They eat dirt!"—but not telling her about the three-fingered boy I was kissing in the woods. At vespers I actually prayed hard to God and on several occasions believed I felt the Holy Spirit enter me then silently cry out and flee. One day after lunch I made an appointment to see Reverend Filo, the camp director. I sat in his office in the back of the main lodge and regarded him steadily. "I want to be baptized," I explained. I didn't know whether he knew about the walks I was taking with his son.

"You haven't been baptized before?"

"No," I lied. It was the last lie, the necessary lie, the great lie to end all lies; the Jesus lie, lying for the sins of all the other lies.

Reverend Filo looked at me. I had no idea what my parents had told him. "You weren't baptized when you were twelve like everyone else?"

"I had mono," I said. The deputy lie. The good-thief-on-the-cross lie. I had been baptized when it meant nothing to me. Now I needed the public atonement—"At-One-ment," as they said here at Camp Panawauc over bug juice and guitar-strummed hymns. I needed the ritual and spectacle. I needed to fall back against a religious man's arms, to be blessed and taken up into the clouds briefly, feel Jesus seize my heart and stay there not shriek and fly off. That hadn't happened the first time. The first time my head had been full of thoughts of breakfast and about how under my baptismal gown, in front of the entire congregation, I wasn't wearing any underwear. Afterward, I'd gleefully eaten donuts and hot chocolate with the other baptismal "candidates," as they were called, while the church ladies dried our hair with towels and a bonnet dryer.

"Well, we should get you baptized, then," said Reverend Filo, as if he were a doctor and this were a perfunctory, snip-and-cut kind of surgery.

Somehow I didn't think I'd be the only one who would be baptized that day, but I was. There were no robes. I wore my bathing suit and a blue linen cape tied in a knot at my throat. I stood with Reverend Filo in waist-high water, a few feet from the dock, little plastic buoys along the side, the lake warm and still and brown in the stagnant way of late summer. There were soft tall weeds growing up from the lake bottom, and they would do a charming kind of hula and then wind around your legs in a death grip.

On shore there was only my counselor, Sandy; Monica Hyde; and Hayden Filo, who smiled at me beneficently. Now I was truly taking his religion and could marry him. Perhaps that's what was crossing his mind. It crossed mine.

"Do you, Benoîte-Marie Carr, accept Jesus as your Lord and Savior?"

These were vows. I summoned forth all the force and promise and devotion I knew I had within me. It formed a large dense mass beneath my ribs. My toes began to cramp and cross. I saw it now: There was only Jesus; everything else was nothing. Everything else was squat. The blue of the sky was endless and beckoning and true. There was Goodness. There was The Way. The mountains across the lake were the apostles, and the trees were witnesses descended from on high. The plastic buoys against the dock were the doves of the Holy Spirit.

"Yes," I said, "I do." Reverend Filo said something else, but I didn't really hear. There were pains and spasms in my feet and legs, and then the Reverend's arm came round the small of my back and he whispered, "Lean back, my dear." I thought of my back dives, squinted my eyes and pushed off with my feet. But I pushed too hard, as if I were doing a real dive, and the leap back brought Reverend Filo staggering back with me. I opened my mouth wide for air, but water rushed in instead, and the weeds wound malignantly around my legs, paralyzing me. My arms clutched and thrashed. I had never been a good swimmer—I could dive but I couldn't swim well; during Swimming at school, with its bathing

suits color-coded to everyone's bust size, I had pretended to
have my period or else early in the morning I'd bang my finger with a hammer until it swelled and I could arrive at the
nurse's office, requesting a splint. So, now, half-drowning,
and bringing a man of God down with me—his head floun-
dering next to mine in the water—I was incapable of saving
myself or anyone. My blue cape billowed out to one side of
me, its knotted ties twisting and tightening around my neck.
I waited for the Holy Spirit to enter me and reside in my
heart in peace, take me forever. I opened my eyes underwater,
where things were silent but full of motion, muddy shapes
and bubbles. I looked up toward the sky and out for God,
but all I saw up through the water was the bright storm on
the sun, and then Sils in her tiara calling my name, and then,
finally, the large looming figure of Frank Morenton, clutching my rope purse—so funny, with my purse!—and looking
down from the clouds, which roiled gassily about his feet and
ankles like large fuzzy slippers. He looked as if he were
scouting out the place, visualizing a turnstile or two and
some rides. There wasn't anything that couldn't use a turnstile! There wasn't anything that couldn't benefit and prosper
from Mr. Amusement! *Mr. Morenton, Mr. Morenton,* I said underwater. *I'm very sorry, Mr. Morenton.* I was near a great and
peaceful death. I felt my soul leave my body yet still retain
the skills of the body, so that I could actually see myself
leave, waving, floating off like a balloon.

And then I was lifted up, coughing, by Reverend Filo
and my counselor, Sandy. "Dear girl!" exclaimed the Reverend, who was also coughing, his hair sopping. "You just
lifted off like a rocket!"

I sat on the shore in my wet cape, and let the sand cake
on it. I coughed some more and spit onto the beach. Monica
Hyde placed towels around me, and Sandy went to get me a

can of soda. Hayden Filo sat next to me, looking disappointed, looking as if that were the most graceless, foolish baptism he'd ever seen.

"Perhaps I can try it again sometime," I croaked.

"Perhaps," he said distantly.

"Let's sing a song, shall we?" said Reverend Filo. And we joined hands in a circle and sang "Jesus Walked This Lonesome Valley." When we got to the last "He had to walk it by himself," Sandy arrived with the soda, and I stepped out of the circle and drank.

At the end of August, before I was sent to the Mount Brookfield School, my mother picked me up at camp to take me home. Getting ready to sit beside her in the car, I had a great desire to be good, a nice girl, like Monica Hyde. But it was when functioning from this desire that I felt most anxious and odd, for what I had was only a desire, not a knack. My mother did not hug me. She asked me if I had everything, and then we got in and stopped first at the nearest gas station, a Sinclair station, its bright green brontosaurus like some reptilian Baby Huey; a puffy, inverted dollar sign. She signaled to the attendant, who was on my side of the car, and as she did I noticed the swaying flesh beneath her bicep and the greenish, black-stubbled oval of her half-shaved underarm—like the prickly, peppery seeds of a tropical fruit. I had to try not to feel repelled by her. I had to remember not her frosty, scolding self, or all the sad, injured love between us, but her niceness, the bursts of energy and originality which she had sometimes bestowed upon me when I was little: sewing new, striped clothes for all my dolls, then arranging them around the room before I woke on Easter; the cakes and breads and frosting bowls she'd leave out for snacks; a dance she once did in my room one night, all by herself, when I was sick in bed and bored. The dance had ended with one of her feet propped on a chair, arms thrust skyward and held like that, her hands clutching two aluminum pie pans. She did have a sense of theater, of costume and set design, and she could make things out of nothing: hats out of rags, doormats out of bottle caps. There were times she fascinated me. But we had never been close, and it was hard for me, ever, to feel I knew her. To know something you had to be able to go inside and feel, then step outside and look, and then do that again: go inside, feel, then outside and look. You had to do it twice. That was knowledge. Two in a row. But with my mother I could only do it once. I'd do it once, the first time, then run.

"Do you feel you learned things at camp?" my mother asked suddenly, after she'd paid the station attendant and pulled away, down the road. She seemed anxious to exude something, some affection; she seemed possessed of some inarticulate goodwill—I could see it surging and flickering in her face, in a kind of confusion.

"Yes," I said.

"Really? That's good. What did you learn?"

What I'd learned at camp, from all the vesper readings, mostly, was that you didn't give back to the same people who gave to you. "Let's see," I said, stalling. You didn't give back to the same people at all. You gave to different people. And they, in turn, gave to someone else entirely. Not you. That was the sloppy economy of gift and love. But that was living as a Christian—a practical Christian, but a Christian nonetheless. This, I realized, my parents already understood. Though it was probably not what they'd hoped I'd learn. "I learned that God is eternal benevolence," I said finally, a little breathlessly.

My mother looked at me with alarm, then became quiet, watching the road. For about forty miles she said nothing,

and then suddenly she started in. "Your grandmother's looking forward to seeing you," she said.

"I'll visit her," I promised.

"Silsby called to find out when you were coming home.
I didn't tell her exactly."

"You didn't?"

"She's not a good influence on you, Berie. She never has
been."

"What do you mean?"

"There's too much strain in her family, the situation with
her parents and all. I always felt you spent too much time
over there. You should have other friends. Her family has
enough to worry about."

"There's strain in every family. Besides, they're not worried about *me*. I'm not getting in the way."

"I'd prefer it if you didn't see her too much right away.
Take a break from the friendship."

"I've *had* a break."

"Silsby and I spoke for a little bit, and I told her the
same thing."

"You did *what*?"

"She said she wasn't going to be around for a week anyway. She was going camping with her boyfriend, Mike, so she
wanted me to tell you that and to wish you all the best at
school, since it looked like she wouldn't be able to see you."

"Wouldn't be able to see me?" Something stung and
ached before my eyes: a picture of Sils, peeling along the lake
roads on the back of the new bike Mike would surely by now
have bought with the insurance money. "The crowd goes
crazy!" he would shout and laugh, whipping dangerously
around the curves. They'd go to the State Park campground,
and in a blue pup tent lie listening to "Brandy, You're a Fine
Girl" on Mike's transistor, slapping the beat on Mike's

thighs. I felt bludgeoned and bleak and abandoned. "Mom, why did you have to say all that?" I bleated mournfully. "You didn't have to say all that!"

"Berie," she said, trying to sound gentle, "you needn't make a tragic caricature of every small emotion." And then we said nothing else, staring straight ahead at the road, or off to the side, where miles of trees had burned in a recent fire— stanch and starch the mush!—and where now toadstools were sprouting through the charred ground.

Back in Horsehearts I went over by myself, on my bicycle, to visit my Grandmother Carr. I had phoned beforehand, and she had suggested the time: two-fifteen.

The weather was cool for August, but I was warm from my bike ride. I climbed wearily up the stairs of her front porch. The door was open, and so I called through the screen. She appeared, wearing a light summer suit, her gray hair curled up in back in a twist. She showed me into her book-lined sitting room, where I had two davenports and a chester-field to choose from. All her furniture was shadowy and hulking, like an indentured household staff. I chose the chesterfield. She brought me a cup of tea. Then she sat down across from me and sipped from her own cup. I looked down at the floor, pretending to study the busy patterns of the Persian rug. I had seldom visited her—I could have counted the times on one hand: the time when I was five and had stood in her kitchen and asked, "Grandma Carr, who is older, you or Daddy?" And she had scowled. *Idiot child!* Or the time when I was seven, and Claude and I brought her a gift—an old jack-in-the-box we didn't want anymore. Or the time when I was ten and brought Sils along, and we sat at the dining table and asked for cookies. My grandmother had fetched us some graham crackers, a little mechanically. "Can we have some juice, too?" I'd asked, and after we departed, full of snacks, she phoned my mother to tell her of our rudeness and demands. When I got home, as punishment, my mother took out all the guest towels and made me iron them.

"Your father tells me you've been in some trouble," my grandmother said now.

I was silent. "A little," I said finally.

"And now they want me to send you to the Mount Brookfield School."

"Yes," I said. I'd forgotten my grandmother would be footing the bill. "I guess."

She looked at me in a vaguely interested way. "Did you enjoy camp?"

"Pretty much," I said.

"Did you?" She looked amused.

"It was interesting to meet all kinds of people from all over the state," I said, like a walking, talking application essay.

She nodded. "We sent your father to camp once," she said. "He was only five years old. At the time he was a little chatterbox, very cute but a chatterbox, and your grandfather and I wanted a vacation alone in Europe." She pursed her mouth and sipped some more tea; I waited to hear a slurp but there wasn't one. "We sent your father to a German summer camp in New Hampshire called Kinder Koop. When he came back, he was stone quiet." She stopped for effect. "He'd become, as he would remain for the rest of his life, a shy person."

The wordless moment now between us was long, low, sonorous as a cello note—a mix of catgut and wood, of animal and plant. "Of course, it was a mistake," she said finally. "It was a terrible, lonely thing we did to such a tiny boy."

Pity pooled in my throat. *Dad!* I drank more tea. I swallowed and coughed.

She now rose from her seat, in a change of subject, and

walked dramatically around the room, as if she were in a play. My eyes followed her, and in so doing, I realized that she had no pictures of us—her children or her grandchildren— anywhere in this room. Nor did she have any elsewhere in the house, that I knew of. "When I was at conservatory," she said, "I'd gone there after much turmoil in my life. To go from turmoil to tranquillity is excellent for music. To go from an iniquitous den to a practice room is a respite given to us by God." She stopped and stared at me. "It is to grow wings. I hope you will find something similar for yourself at the Mount Brookfield School."

"I hope so, too," I said. "I mean, I don't see why not."

"Well, my dear . . ." She was still standing; she had already put her teacup down. Now she looked at her watch. "I realize you have many things to do. But I wish you all the best." I stood up, as I guessed I was supposed to, though I still had half a cup of tea. She shook my hand and kissed me on the cheek. Suddenly I loved her very much.

"Thank you," I said. I threw my arms around her waist and hugged her tightly. I pressed my right cheek against the pale lapels of her suit and closed my eyes. "I hope I'll have a musical moment like that, too," I said awkwardly, and she made a light, humming sound like a laugh and patted me on the head.

At the Mount Brookfield School I wrote to everyone: to Hayden Filo, to Claude, to my parents. I wrote to my grand-mother. "Hey, Grams," I began one letter, but then crossed it out and wrote "Dear Grandmother Carr." By the cross-out I drew an arrow and wrote "picture of me in a new hat." She never wrote back.

But my parents did. They said they had given my room to a Japanese foreign student and weren't sure whether there'd be room for me to come home either fall break or Thanksgiving, though Christmas was fine.

To Sils I wrote long descriptions of the "precious, pukey campus," of all my difficult schoolwork, of the dining hall where dogs were allowed and there was unlimited ice cream (the eccentric demands of some benefactor). I described the native attire, the preppie Scottish sweaters I refused to buy, though once I almost hocked one in town but put it back.

I dressed in what I thought was glamorous—black and gold things. Sometimes a cape or a hat or a scarf that sparkled. I arranged my face and hair in a fever of private notions: a theater of one. I wasn't looking around. I wasn't costuming myself in any context that was real. If I pushed it too far, if it got too glittery or tacky, I'd say to people, "Hey, at Horsehearts High *this* is *chic.*" I'd send it all up as a joke, a put-on. But if it seemed to work, if people liked it, I would say, "Thank you," in an earnest, whispered way. I became exotic among the preppies. I hung out with the wisecracking boys.

I got my period. The torrent of it, the bodily upheaval, filled me with happiness and dread. In drugstores I stared at the Modess and Kotex and belts and equipment, obsessed with the paraphernalia. I made directly for the back aisles and hovered there, like a robber, waiting for a slow moment in the store. I remained there in a kind of hypnosis, until something would snap me out of it, and I would wander back out, via the perfume counter, where I would spray all the testers—on my wrists, behind my ears—then step outside and get attacked by bees.

I got good grades. I learned to use the words "nebulous" and "juxtaposition," and tried to use them as often as I could: in essay tests, or just standing in line at the dining hall.

I won an academic prize.

I developed breasts.

For a while I was still telling my flat-chested jokes. But as my own breasts grew larger, so did the disjunction between my body and my jokes, and when I would tell jokes to people, they would look at me funny. I was in a time warp. My breasts had become larger—they were large!—and I was still referring to them as mosquito bites. For a semester, an embarrassing, amphibious semester when I didn't know who I was, what I looked like, what jokes to tell, moving from water to land, I tried to stop telling any jokes at all. I waited until I'd accumulated enough amusing lines about having *big* breasts, armed myself with enough invented descriptions, amassed enough self-deprecating remarks about top-heaviness— knockers, blimps, hooters, bazooms—to get me through a party, and then I told those. Getting stuck in elevators, toppling forward, not being able to see the forest for the cleavage. Alienated in a grotesque way, I would stagger forward in a kind of list, then rest my breasts on the nearest bookcase. I was doing sight gags. I didn't care. In not caring, I became the same as everyone else: I was waiting to go far away to a big university, away from this woodsy dumping ground for half-loved kids, off to a big university that would be Relevant and Real.

But then I got my first boyfriend, a boy named Howie March. I'd met him in the Linen Service line, where we were waiting together to pick up our neat little papered bundles and drop off our old sheets like invalids or mental patients or old people in a home. Howie was on the wrestling team— passionate and obsessive and sweet. He liked me. I would go to his matches and tournaments wearing my funny little black-and-gold hats and smoking my cigarettes outside in the hallway, and afterward he would give me his trophies, little metal men with arms protruding in a starting stance, and I would take them back to my dorm room and hang my jewelry on them. I loved him fiercely, like an orphan, with every newly banished, bereaved, and sexual part of me. I had no idea who either of us was; there was just the thick fog of love and bodies and whispered promises. We were child bride, child groom, each seeking the other's animal heart. He would make love to me slow, fast, against the wall, standing up. His naked body—its power and vulnerability, the steely arms, his penis with its delicate veins like the veins of a wrist, its rubbery eye like the tip of a mucilage bottle—obsessed me. I developed a blush. Before then, I had never blushed. I didn't have the body fat, the heat, the hormones, the awareness of myself, the belief in my own visibility that would have created a blush. But now I'd become a sexual creature with all its experience of shame and being watched. The dark, sallow circles beneath my eyes disappeared in a pale bloat, my glance was less direct, and I began to blush easily, daily. I blushed for years.

In letters to Sils I would write "I miss you!" "How are you, schweetie?" and then I would tell her about Howie: a *dunk*, half dork, half hunk. "He keeps me busy!" I would write. "Wink, wink." And then I'd draw a picture of a wink.

The few times I went home on vacations, I would see Sils, but we were strangely awkward with each other. We looked different. She had layered her hair in a long wavy shag and was wearing a big leather jacket and palazzo pants. I had grown rounded and tall. We would sing in her room, but at the end of a song she'd strum the chords and we'd retreat shyly into silence. We didn't reprise our repertoire, all the songs we'd learned with Miss Field in Girls' Choir, or from the car radio, or her brothers' band. Instead we struggled with talk, though it all seemed to separate us. She had broken up with Mike and was now seeing a boy named Doug, who sold mobile homes. Months before, her brothers had once again fled, with their band, to Canada. Was I going to college? She thought she might not, but might just stay in town and work for the post office or something. Someday she hoped to move to Boston or Hawaii or Santa Fe.

"Oh," I said. I'd somehow always thought we'd go to college together, to the same place; I couldn't imagine being totally without her.

"There's just no money," she said. But she smiled at me encouragingly, like an older sister.

"No prob," I said. "No biggie. I can get the cash. I can do this thing with ticket stubs." I hoped she would laugh. Instead she smiled weakly and ran her fingers through her new hair. She seemed tired and sad and it made me want to run, to be gone, to be back at Mount Brookfield with Howie.

I was Howie's girlfriend for a year, before he left, graduated from Mount Brookfield ahead of me, and bucking his parents, set out with two buddies for the Alaskan pipeline, where after three months, I was told later by his mother, he disappeared in the snow, came down with the snow madness that caused men to get into their tractors and just drive off into the blinding white horizon, never coming back.

I forced myself to go on to someone else after that, then someone else again, never attaching in quite the same ferocious, virginal way, never with that enthralled and orphaned heart, not quite like that, and I missed him for years, years into college. By then my parents had moved from Horsehearts to the east coast of Florida with my grandmother, who, when I visited, stared at me with the staggering, arrogant stare of the dying, the wise vapidity of the already gone; she refused to occupy the features of her face. The living didn't interest her; she grew bored when anyone spoke. In her yawn I could see the black-and-white dice of her filled teeth, the quiet snap of her spit, all gathered in a painting of departure. It is unacceptable, all the stunned and anxious missing a person is asked to endure in life. It is not to be endured, not really.

———

AFTER COLLEGE, I did go back to Horsehearts, for a class reunion. Ten years. I was invited despite the Mount Brookfield diploma—"a mere technicality," wrote Susie Vito, the class secretary, who had been in kindergarten with me. Sils wrote me a note: "If you go, I'll go," she said. "The reunion's at a motel. But please stay with me at my house. I've got room." She was still in Horsehearts, renting cheaply, working as a letter carrier and putting in requests for transfers. Her handwriting was exactly the same, jazzy and elegant, with *f*s that looked like G clefs. *S*s like flowers.

Like so many others, I arrived by car, still smoking cigarettes, my hair shorn, some money and credit cards in my purse. How simple and sweet and nice Sils seemed then, at that befuddled gathering! She ran toward me and hugged me so long I felt abandoned when she let go. Her face was slightly lined—there were deeper folds by her mouth—but otherwise she looked the same. It was her! "Your hair looks great," she said, and took my hand. How kind she was! She was a lovely and gentle person, and I'd almost forgotten. I had gone out into the world and in it imagined *myself* sweet and good compared to the jagged acrimony I met everywhere. "I'm just a girl from Horsehearts, what can I say?" I'd murmur, and men would touch my face; New Yorkers, Bostonians, Parisians would smile. But now, returning to Horsehearts, I realized, I no longer knew what sweetness was. By comparison to what I found there, I had become sour, mean, sophisticated. I no longer knew from niceness, was no longer on a daily basis with it. I didn't meet nice people. I met witty, hard, capable, successful, dramatic. Some vulnerable. Some insecure. But not nice, the way Sils was nice. She was nice the way I had long imagined I still was, but then on see-ing her again—strangely shy before me but illumined and grinning, as ever, her voice in gentle girlish tones I never heard anymore—instantly, completely, knew I was no longer.

We jumped into the motel pool, with our clothes on, laughing and practically drowning. We swam together to the shallow end, and when she stepped out of it, gleaming, her clothes wet and tight as leather, her hair streaming down her back, everyone looked. Though there was weariness in her walk, she was still slender and bold; I could see she was still some kind of sexual centerpiece here. All the Horsehearts boys who had stayed in town, become managers of stores or cinemas or the roller rink, still thought of her at night. In this neck of the woods, she was the neck of the woods.

We sat in lawn chairs, drying in the sun, and smoked quietly, with Randi, who seemed just the same as always except that, recovered from her Mary Kay days, she had changed her name to Travis, which she'd written on her name tag, with Randi in parentheses underneath. (Could one do that? Could one put one's whole past, the fact of its boring turbulence, in parentheses like that?) We murmured about how bald all the boys were. "They look exactly like they did in high school," said Sils, "except that now their hair's gone and in their wallets instead of condoms they carry before-and-after photos of their home renovations. Welcome back to Horsehearts." As she held her cigarette, and blew smoke away from me, I looked for the men from *U.N.C.L.E.* in her toe-nails but could not find them.

After the afternoon reception and buffet, we left, went to

go drink in a new local restaurant, what Sils called "an-all-you-will-have-eaten place." There was a long salad bar and a big open grill. One was supposed to cook one's own steak. "Cook your own mistake," she called it. I smiled in a way that I hoped wouldn't seem distant. What did it mean that she had stayed here, in Horsehearts, in one place, like a tree? Though I knew one's roots grew deep and steady that way, still, one's lower limbs could fuse, or die, killed off by one's own stalwart shade. "It's the coleslaw here," she said. "I just can't get enough of it. Sometimes I think that, you know, watch: the slaw alone will keep me in this town forever."

Later, she drove me around the village, to show me it again. The yards seemed emptier and larger than I remembered, the houses farther apart and glum, though pretty. A couple of times we got out and walked. There was no one on the street. The old sidewalks sparkled with quartz until we hit a part that had been repaired or replaced with newer clayey squares. When we drove by my old house, it seemed ungainly and obscene in its strangeness; in my mind the proportions of the house were warmer, different; in my mind it wasn't *this*. It seemed alien. It seemed confiscated. "Let's get out of here," I said. The roads were country roads, still wooded and full of longing and despair and that search for something, anything going on; they were roads of rumor—curvy, restless roads that seemed for moments to stretch forward but then just turned back in on themselves, like snakes snacking on their own tails.

Back at her house, in the cool snap of the Adirondack night, Sils and I got into pajamas and collapsed sleepily on her water bed, which was heated and huge, a thing I might have found tasteless somewhere else but here was some perfection of calm and form, a dead man's float on still water, while she spoke of getting a postal route in Hawaii.

"You can do that?" I asked.

"Sure." She spoke some more of her life here, its trapped routines. Her mother had died. "She slaved away at that motel, and then she just died, without ever even a postcard from my dad." Her brothers had moved to Texas and formed a band called the Jackhammer Hamsters. "Ever heard of them?"

"I'm not sure," I said.

"They're getting a little *old*," she whispered, and offered up a gentle wince.

She loved Hawaii. She'd been there once—with a guy named Mel—and had bought a big coffee-table book called *Hawaiian Song* in the airport. She got up from the bed to fetch it, spread it out on the billowing quilt, showed me some of the photographs: bright beaches and skies. Not an Adirondack in sight. "I've been on a postal transfer list for three years," she said.

"It's just a matter of time, then."

"Probably."

"Gee." I sighed.

"Yeah." She smiled in a bittersweet way.

I browsed through my mind, thinking about all the things I wanted to say, might say, could say. "Guess what?"

"What? I don't know!"

"I'm engaged."

"Get out of town! You are?" she exclaimed eagerly. "Where's your ring!"

"We're doing a cheap and easy minimalist thing: no rings, no wedding. Just—marriage." I sighed.

"How Modern!"

"Yeah. Instead of saying 'I do,' we're just going to say 'Here.' "

"And what's Mr. Here's name?"

"Daniel Hiawatha Bergman."

"That's his real name? Get out!"

"I swear to God."

"Is he a good guy?"

A good guy. It sounded so Martha and the Vandellas. But
it was Horsehearts. That was the way Horsehearts sounded.
"Yeah. He's a good guy."

"Great, Berie, I'm so happy for you. You deserve a good
guy." Now she sighed. "And I always knew you'd get one. I always thought you'd end up with the best husband of all of us."

"You did?"

"Of course. You had no idea. But of course."

For a fleeting moment, as anyone can, I imagined I felt
the poverty of my future, all its unholdable surfaces; I felt in-
explicably ungrateful and sad. It was a moment of stillness in
which one looks around and ruefully sees only the rocks and
searing sun and cheap metal. "You wanted an adventure and
instead you got Adventureland," Sils herself used to say. I
longed for a feeling again, a particular one: the one of ap-
proaching a room but of not yet having entered it. Being engaged to marry, it should have been what I felt. But instead
I associated the feeling with another part of my life: that
anteroom of girlhood, with its laughter as yet only affianced
to the world, anticipation playing in the heart like an orches-
tra tuning and warming, the notes unwed and fabulous and
crazed—I wanted it back!—those beginning sounds, so much
more interesting than the piece itself.

Pièce—French for room, I remembered, the strangeness of
night and this one upon me like a drug.

"You guys going to have kids?" asked Sils. She wriggled
her way under the covers.

"Sure," I said. "Why not?"

"That's great," she said. But something haggard suddenly

entered her face. "That's great." She gave a yawn. "I suppose we should go to sleep."

"It's been a long day."

"Good night, Berie," she said, turning out the light. In the dark she added, "Congratulations! Thank you. I love you." She paused. "Is there anything I missed?"

"Good luck," I said. "Drive safely. Wipe your feet. Happy Birthday and Have a Nice Life. There's a lot you forgot."

"Many happy returns," she said sleepily. "And Good Fate. That's the real one." She turned with the sheet clutched to her breastbone, the water beneath us rolling gently. I lay in the dark next to her, feeling like a creature that had entered through a damp cranny or a bad shingle in the roof: a bat that could swoop silently about in her house. Why not? Bats, I knew, were sentimental. They returned to where they once lived, even when shut out; they sought their own smell. I couldn't sleep. I was lying on top of the covers, which made it easy to get up. I rolled out of bed, stepped ashore, out into her house, and roamed through the rooms, touching things. I couldn't really see what they were, but I could feel them: a needlepoint pillow, a pile of newsprint shoppers, little ceramic statues of cats—discovering these cats, I felt less shocked than puzzled and disappointed—a large, foil-wrapped chocolate egg, a basket of hair ties and barrettes.

I went into the bathroom. I touched the towels and towel bars and washcloths. I flicked on the light and opened the medicine cabinet: Q-Tips, nail files, and dark beeswax soaps. I opened the pill bottles and took an aspirin and a Tylenol. I dabbed cologne on my wrists, stripped naked, then got into the shower, where I washed my hair with her shampoo—an apricot-walnut one that smelled like her. I stayed there for a long time—used her back scrub brush and her creme rinse and let the bathroom fog up with steam. I lathered myself with a muddy scrap of beeswax soap I clawed out of the shower caddy. I felt close to her, in a larcenous way, as if here in the shower, using her things, all the new toiletries she now owned, I could know better the person she'd become. All evening I'd been full of reminiscences, but she had seldom joined in. Instead she was full of kindnesses—draping her own sweater around my shoulders, bringing me tea. How could I know or hope that she contained within her all our shared life, that she had not set it aside to make room for other days and affections and things that now had all made their residence and marks within her? Of course, I knew there were no reassurances. Or, there were only reassurances. She had offered them. "This place is just not the same without you," she had said twice that afternoon. But I was greedy. Three was the magic number. I'd wanted her to say it one more time.

I got out, wrapped a towel around me, and went back to bed, where she lay still asleep, curved in a pale paisley, the sheet about her like an old tricot curtain. I slipped quietly under the covers, my hair wet, feeling the water bed give slightly beneath me like something gelatinous and alive.

"Did you just take a *shower?*" Sils suddenly murmured, surprising me.

"Yeah, I did."

She kept her eyes closed, and simply readjusted her pillow for sleep. "You were always a weird girl," she said dreamily.

"I was?" I said. "I was not."

She gave a lazy laugh. "You should invite me to where you live someday and see all the wacky things I'm going to do."

"I will," I said. "I will." Though I already imagined that by the time I got back to my new job and life, with all its distractions and busynesses, that I wouldn't know how. Or why. Despite all my curatorial impulses and training, my priestly harborings and professional, courtly suit of the past, I never knew what to do with all those years of one's life: trot around in them forever like old boots—or sever them, let them fly free?

Of course, one couldn't really do either. But there was always the trying, and pretending. And then there was finally someplace in between, where one lived.

I curled next to Sils and closed my eyes. I slept the light, watery sleep of a sick person who has already slept off the day and then awakened to night, not knowing what to do.

In the morning, she brought me coffee. She brought me a salad.

"This is the best salad I've ever had," I said. For a brief moment, I decided, I would defeat nostalgia with caffeine. "This is better than all the others. This is the best salad of my entire life."

"It's the dressing," she said. "A kind of breakfast recipe: it actually has bacon and eggs in it." She shrugged and smiled.

I set my coffee aside. "Do you play the guitar anymore?" I asked.

"Only some," she said.

"Do you still paint?"

"Naw." She waved her hand dismissively. "Well, oh, I painted *one* thing," she said, and she went out on the sunporch and brought back a small canvas on which she'd painted a bowl of fruit. In the painting of the bowl, which was silver, she'd included a reflection of a tiny figure of a woman, head into the wind, hair blown back. "That's me getting ready to face middle age," she said. And we both laughed in a loud, delirious way.

She was, probably, the nicest person I had ever known.

Yet in the years following, for myself, I abandoned even be-
lieving in niceness or being nice. I could scarcely control myself, wherever I was, from telling everyone, anyone, what I
thought of them. It was an urge, a compulsion, my tongue
bitten a futile blue. *That's a ridiculous thing to say. You must
have been spoiled as a child.* I couldn't stop myself. *You are un-
generous. You parcel yourself out like an expensive spice. You idealize
things; you're a narcissist. You seek only to etch impressions of yourself on someone else's face. It's a form of cheapness. You're cheap.
You're patronizing. You're a fascist. You're a bully. I've always
hated bullies. You look awful in that color.* It was as if I'd been
hit on the head.

I left before noon. Sils walked me out to my car and gave
me a long hug. "Aw, Berie," she said, "how'd we get so old
and far away," and then she stepped backward, turning, and
walked to the front porch, from where she turned again
and waved. "I'm going to get a dog," she said; certainly that
was all that was needed to complete the scene.

"Sounds good," I said stupidly. I started the car.

"Good luck with the Historical Society—whatever the
hell it is you do there," she called out.

"Photography curator. I organize old pictures," I called
back.

"That's right," she said. "Well, organize those pictures,
girl!" She shook a fist and laughed. Then she brushed some
hair off her brow and folded her arms across her chest. Her
smile was broad at first, then tightened into something perfunctory. Perhaps she was suddenly embarrassed, as a woman,
of what we had been to each other as girls. I waved again and
honked my horn loudly, all the way down the street, under
the canopy of summer trees and out into the main streets of
Horsehearts.

· · ·

I drove west five miles to a restaurant called the Horsehearts Country Restaurant. I was supposed to have lunch with LaRoue. "Go see LaRoue," my mother had said. "She's been depressed and calling us for money." She had not moved to Florida with my parents, but had stayed north to work grooming fillies at the racetrack. She also worked sometimes as a janitor for a restaurant. Just for today she would get the owner of the restaurant to pay her in food. "A meal for me and my sister!" she'd exclaimed on the phone in a way that alarmed me. Her teeth had fallen out, and her dentures hurt her, so she didn't wear them, she said, warning me in advance on the phone.

She was waiting for me in the restaurant foyer. She'd grown even heavier and her smile was more tentative but also wilder in its red, toothless spread. Her short, corn-colored hair sat like a cap on her head, but it seemed patchy, and was shaved at the nape. She came forward and hugged me, and with one thick arm still around me, she showed me to our table. Her nails, I noticed, had been bitten so low they looked like ragged bits of shell inlaid in her fingers. Her cuticles were grimy and frayed.

"So how've you been!" she kept saying when we were seated. "Order anything you want!"

Creamed chicken specials, plates of fried vegetables, cheese sandwiches with soup. It was hard to think of all the ways you'd never come through for people, closed them out, never loved them, and still order lunch. "It's difficult to decide," I said.

"Order anything! I've got this. I've got this taken care of." She smiled.

"Are you sure?"

"Of course! I've been really looking forward to this!"

"You have? That's really nice."

"Honest to God, Berie. It's true; I've missed you. I think of you and say, 'What is that girl up to? I need to buy her lunch. I need to buy her anything she wants off the menu.'"

When, three years later, LaRoue hung herself in the county hospital psychiatric ward, the nurses arriving too late to cut her down, I would remember this exuberance, the hollow nervousness and yet the genuine sororal note, rattling around there, trying to get out.

Probably I was a little formal. "Well, thanks," I said. Though I longed to do something now, as her foster sister, I had done nothing for LaRoue, ever. All I'd ever wanted was to be with Sils. An act of substitution, as maybe love always was. The world with its thinkers and refugees and difficult news had come to my doorstep, as best it could, for short visits—Mr. Sabeke from the Congo, say, or José Meyers from Argentina—they had all come to our house, people just out of prison (a *fellow* or a *felon*? I'd asked a man named Ed Stedson, when I was ten, and he had laughed uproariously from his Hide-A-Bed), people came to us, orphaned and in need, like LaRoue, but all I'd wanted was my friend Sils, who would stay with me in my room and smile and smoke, keep the busy, roaring strange-tongued world at bay. In this, even if this were all, she could never become boring. If she lived where I lived then, at the moment, that was enough. If we spoke on the phone every night. If no one else came along, a visitor with snake oil and demands, to complicate our girlhood, it might stretch before us like a lovely beach. I'd wanted no other constructions. Only the simple, purgatorial life we had.

For LaRoue, I'd done nothing.

"I hope you don't ever hold anything against me from when we were kids," LaRoue said now. It shocked me.

"What things?" I asked.

"Oh, I don't know. I look back, and it seems I was pretty mean to you and Claude."

"You weren't mean."

"Well, thanks for saying that," she said.

"No. I *mean* it."

"You weren't *mean*. I *mean* it," she chanted, and started laughing nervously. "See that table over there? I had to vacuum under it this morning and guess what I found?"

"What?"

"Money," she said, as if this were a secret I especially would appreciate.

"Good," I said. "How much?"

"A five."

"Great," I said, though I wished for her sake it had been a twenty.

I ordered chicken salad, and she ordered soup and a soft muffin. We talked about my parents, about Claude doing so well with his computer business in Baltimore, about dogs and fillies and jockeys. We talked about Horsehearts and how the place was fifteen years ago. "You and Silsby Chaussée," she said. "You guys were inseparable; it was the talk of the town."

"It was?"

"Well, sort of. Now it would take a lot more than that to get the town talking."

I smiled, tried to enjoy myself. "Yeah, like what?"

"Like a convention center," she said, and we both laughed loudly.

When we finished eating, the check never came to the table. We waited, then got up, walked out of the dining room, and in the lobby she introduced me to the owner of the restaurant, a big, hale and hearty type who put his arm around LaRoue in an affectionate way. It seemed nice, the way he was with her, and at that moment, for a split second, she seemed happy.

"You were up here for your class reunion?" he asked me.

"That, and to see LaRoue," I said. I lied.

"Those can be something, those reunions," he said.

"You're on your hundredth," LaRoue said, flirting with him in this provincial, teasing way.

"Hundred and fiftieth!" he exclaimed. "Reunions," he mused. "They just keep coming at you, and what can you do?"

"That's true," I said. "What can you do?"

"Well, it was a pleasure to meet you," he replied, and shook my hand. He patted LaRoue on the back. "Lunch is on me." When he left, I could see that she was worried about something.

"Are you OK?" I asked.

"Yeah. Sure."

I had three hundred miles of driving ahead. "It was good to see you, LaRoue," I said. I kissed her, threw my arms around her, taking in the big, ugly helplessness of her. Then I got in the car.

"You take care," she said. "You take care of yourself."

Driving alone along the Northway, feeling more haunted than I really had the courage to be, I cried in the car the way one does when leaving someone in a bitter and unbearable way. I don't know why I should have picked that time to grieve, to summon everything before me—my own monstrousness, my two-bit affections, three-bit, four. It could have been sooner, it could have been later, it could have been one of the hot, awkward funerals (my grandmother's, LaRoue's, my father who one morning in Vero Beach clutched his fiery arm and fell dead off his chair mouthing to my mother, "Help. Heart. I love you"—how every death makes the world a lonelier place), it could have been some other time when the sun wasn't so bright, and there was no news on the radio, and my arms were not laced in a bird's nest on the steering wheel, my life going well, I believed, pretty well. It could have been any other time. But it was then: I cried for Sils and LaRoue, all that devotion and remorse, stars streaming light a million years after dying; I cried for the boyfriends I was no longer with, the people and places I no longer knew very well, for my parents and grandmother ailing and stuck in Florida, their tough, unchanging forms conjured only in memory: a jewel box kept in a medicine cabinet in the attic of a house on the moon; that's where their unchanging forms were kept. I cried for everyone and for all the scrabbly, funny love one sent out into the world like some hit song that enters space and bounds off to another galaxy, a tune so pretty you think the words are true, you do! There was never any containing a song like that, keeping it. It went off and out, speeding out of earshot or imagining or any reach at all, like a rocket invented in sleep.

The next reunion, after that, five years later, Sils didn't come, but sent flowers from Hawaii instead: *To the class of '74. Much love, Sils Chaussée.* And after that I, too, sent flowers, and a note, and didn't show up anymore.

YOU CAN wake from one dream only to find yourself plunged into yet another, like some endless rosary of the mind. When that happens, it is hard to glimpse what is not dream; the waking, undreamed world flies by you, in rushing flashes of light and air, in loud, quick, dangerous spaces like those between the cars of a train. There is nothing you can do. You walk in the sleep of yourself and wait. You wait for the train to pass.

Daniel believes he is working something out, wrestling with his heart, his work. He wants me to bear with him. He speaks in a coded way of all that is tempting and bewildering him, all issues of moral drunkenness. "It's like I'm on a ride," he says. "I go up, up, and up, and then *wheeeee.*"

"Except then the keys fall out of your pocket," I say sternly. "And then you can't get back into the house."

He tries to look bemused. "I had a dream last night that I rounded a corner and someone lifted a gun and shot me, the bullet slamming straight through my sternum." He pauses. "Do you think that's bad luck?" He sighs, then begins to whisper. "I'm afraid of one day turning into my father. When he was my age, he left my mother for a woman twenty years younger."

I say nothing. I melt a whiskey truffle on my tongue. In my vision there are lines running through everything; even the fabric of the drapes and upholstery seem to be raining, like the clothes in a portrait by van Gogh.

Daniel looks sad, draws his large man's hand down across his face; his voice constricts with sorrow. "My mother, of course, took it with the great good humor with which it was intended."

"She lost her mind," I say.

"Yes," he says. "She lost her mind."

Eating brains—their spongy circuitry reabsorbed—we pretend is an ecological act. But perhaps it is more like monsters in a science fiction movie. Brains! Brains! Brains! As if we have run out of our own. So far in our marriage we've fought fear with ineptitude, indifference with indifference; the world blows up here and there, and our lives feel staked out in the embers, pitched and huddled in tents. We course through the hairpin turns of denials and shouts—it's the end, it can't be the end—we are in the loveliest city in the world: the expensive coffees, the red chemical sunset, the *bateaux mouches* flashing by each sooty church, lighting it up like a stage. In *salons de thé* the waiters set the crêpes aflame with

Bic Flics pulled brusquely from their shirt pockets. The gendarmes hassle the African men in the *métro*; the poodles defecate with impunity on the walks. You can't name your child anything not on a national list—and this is the most civilized city on earth! The city of spring and songs and other compositions of the heart. We feel ourselves moving so minusculely against some process, some momentum, that we become inadvertently a part. We feel too small to fight. Desperation, laziness, horror—they all resemble one another in their flickering movements within us, the same thrashing shorthand. *Ma chérie, is this our stop?* We feel enslaved—is that what it is?—in some turning: of milk to rot to dirt and winds and then to what—to sleep? to stars? Time for another constellation!

My husband has that look again, the look of how difficult the world is, life is, how sometimes you just want to go back to your house with the bushes around it and stay inside.

"Home," he says. The idea of it: its lovely cheat and evasion; its capitulation to longing and rest. "Home, home, home."

Where, though I harbor secret wishes of its burning, our life in flames, the crazy, wicked freedom of it, our chipping house will still be standing, safe and whole, the previous owner's rubber bands still wrapped around the doorknobs. The animals we've sealed in, in mending and patching—the mice and larks—will wake and cry within the walls, then go still. The season will be spring, but the squirrels will have eaten and rearranged the bulbs, so that only one lone daffodil—a trumpet solo!—will be shivering in the yard, the flowering quince not flowering, the ground still too muddy for grass but on a sunny day ticking with hatching flies. At the Citgo station around the corner the sparrows will once again build their nest in the paper towel dispenser. "Don't you feel, you must, like going home?" Daniel asks in a voice of such ailing homesickness it makes me smile.

Everywhere life is full of heroism.

I lean warmly toward him, try to get closer, in empathy and companionship, to study his face, so moist and young in these rains, to match or approximate it. "Don't be lorn, don't be blue, it's only morn, and I'm with you." I sing this, but he stiffens, then tries not to stiffen, forces a smile but moves too quickly away. He does this often now. Something, someone, keeps him, is kept, in some other corner of his life. I can't follow him there—where that is, a place of woundedness, we are too without each other. To meet there would be to step into the strange dark rage of strangers. But I've accrued a kind of patience, I believe, loosely like change. I can feel the jangle and money of it. I will wait for him, I think: let him go and sicken himself, confuse himself, dash through the bad woods of himself. *Love is perennial as the grass!* I'll wait for him, my heart in epilogue, knit and reknit, perhaps as it always has been. I'll wait until I just can't wait anymore.

As far as possible, without surrender, be on good terms with all persons.

———

THERE WAS an April afternoon, when I was in the tenth grade, that the Girls' Choir had to meet for its final rehearsal before the spring concert. The sun was pouring in through the gym windows, and when we took our places on the bleachers we were standing in it, like something celestial lowered in. Our director, Miss Field, began to wave her arms at us, and a strange spell came over our throats. Our nerves tightened and all the bones of our ears fell in line. It was Miss Field's own arrangement of a Schubert rhapsody, and the notes, for once, took flight. I didn't, couldn't, catch Sils's eye—she was standing over with the sopranos—but it didn't matter, I didn't have to, because this wasn't personal, this singing, this light, this was girls, after weeks of rehearsal, celebrating the ethereal work of their voices, the bell-like, birdlike, child-sound they could still make so strongly in unison. Strung along the same wire of song, we lost ourselves; out of separate rose and lavender mouths we formed a single living thing, like a hyacinth. It seemed even then a valedictory chorus to our childhood and struck us deep in the brain and low in the spine, like a call, and in its wave and swell lifted us, I swear, to the ceiling in astonishment and bliss, we sounded that beautiful. All of us could hear it, aloft in the midst of it, no boys, no parents in the room, no one else to tell us, though we never managed to sound that beautiful again. In all my life as a woman—which began soon after and not unrichly—I have never known such a moment. Though sometimes in my brain I go back to that afternoon, to relive it, sail up there again toward the acoustic panels, the basketball hoops, and the old oak clock, the careful harmonies set loose from our voices so pure and exact and light we wondered later, packing up to leave, how high and fast and far they had gone.

A NOTE ON THE TYPE

The text of this book was set in Garamond, a modern rendering of the type first cut by Claude Garamond (c. 1480–1561). Garamond was a pupil of Geoffroy Tory and is believed to have based his letters on the Venetian models, although he introduced a number of important differences, and it is to him we owe the letter which we know as "old style." He gave to his letters a certain elegance and a feeling of movement that won for their creator an immediate reputation and the patronage of Francis I of France.

Composed by Creative Graphics, Inc.,
Allentown, Pennsylvania

Printed and bound by Arcata Graphics/Martinsburg,
Martinsburg, West Virginia

Designed by Dorothy S. Baker